The Lonely Crossing of Juan Cabrera

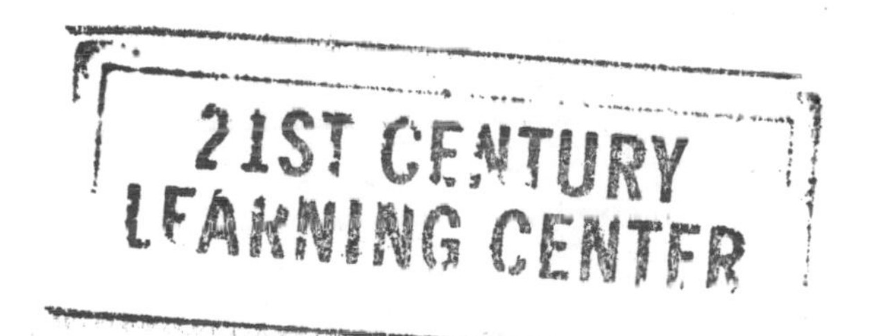

J. Joaquín Fraxedas

The Lonely Crossing of Juan Cabrera

St. Martin's Press

NEW YORK

 For information, address St. Martin's Press, 175 Fifth Avenue, New York, N.Y. 10010.

Design by BARBARA M. BACHMAN
Production Editor: SUZANNE MAGIDA

Library of Congress Cataloging-in-Publication Data
Fraxedas, J. Joaquín
The lonely crossing of Juan Cabrera / J. Joaquín Fraxedas.
p. cm.
ISBN 0-312-08897-3 (hardcover)
ISBN 0-312-11022-7 (paperback)
1. Cuban Americans—Fiction. I. Title.
PS3566.R3567L66 1993
813'.54—dc20 92-40821
CIP

First Paperback Edition: May 1994

10 9 8 7 6 5 4 3

To my mother

To my second mother, María del Carmen Cueto

and

To the memory of my father

"Freedom, Sancho, is one of the
most precious gifts that Heaven
has bestowed upon men; no treasures
that the earth holds buried or
the sea conceals can compare with
it; for freedom, as for honor,
life may and should be ventured."

—CERVANTES, *Don Quixote,*
PART II, CHAPTER 58

The wind that always blows from the east, off the coast of Africa, strokes the warm surface of the tropical Atlantic. The water yields to the constant wind and follows it westward across the ocean. At first the water travels in two parallel currents, the north equatorial and the south equatorial. But as these twin currents sweep into the Caribbean Sea they join to become one great stream that skirts the islands of the Lesser Antilles, rebounds off the Central American coast, and returns to the Atlantic through the Straits of Florida with the power of a thousand Mississippis.

At the narrowest part of the Straits, where the flow is strongest, the stream passes by the ancient port city of Havana before turning north toward the east coast of

Florida. This turn to the north, and the carrying power of its currents, has made this stream at once the corridor and the moving force of a long and watery exodus from the island of Cuba.

*"You shall not stay here grieving . . .
go, cut some beams of wood, and make
yourself a large raft with an upper
deck that it may carry you safely over
the sea."*

—HOMER, *the Odyssey,*
BOOK V

The Lonely Crossing of Juan Cabrera

Chapter *One*

Driving back to Havana after delivering his lecture at the University of Camagüey, Professor Juan Cabrera took one last detour, looking for a fragment of a past that for thirty years he had pretended never existed. Forty kilometers west of the city of Camagüey he left the central highway that runs the length of the island and, after several wrong turns, managed to find his way to a dirt road that cut through sugarcane fields that were once part of the Santa Cruz, the old Cabrera family estate.

The spacious country house with its arched floor-to-ceiling windows, which his grandfather had built around the turn of the century, was gone now, along with all the outbuildings. The framboyán trees that had shaded and cooled the area around the great house in midsummers, and graced the yard in golden afternoons with their carpets of orange flowers, had all been cut down.

After the revolution, everything had been razed and later replaced by a series of long, barracks-style structures made of cinder blocks with corrugated zinc roofs. The barracks housed the sugar cutters in what was now a collective labor camp during the *zafra,* the time of the sugarcane harvest. But it would be four months before the *zafra* started, and today the camp was deserted.

Professor Cabrera stopped his car and walked toward the place where his home had once been. He looked for a trace of the foundation, for a rock from the old well, for some remnant of the flagstones lining the walks that had connected the main house with the other buildings on the property. Everything had disappeared. They had taken obvious care to leave nothing behind that would serve as a reminder of what had once been a splendid estate.

Juan remembered riding his tricycle, bumping along the flagstone paths, following his father to the stables where he would climb aboard an elaborately carved antique carriage bearing the Cabrera family crest. His grandfather, Don Francisco, had bought the carriage in Barcelona in 1901 and sent it to Cuba as a concession to Juan's grandmother, Doña Pepa, before relocating his family, his fortune, and the collective fate of his posterity to the wild tropics.

Doña Pepa had protested, "Cuba is a savage place, full of flies and convicts." But there was no dissuading Don Francisco, who had amassed a fortune selling the latest English bathroom fixtures all over Spain, and had even managed to land the toilet concession at the 1888 World's Fair in Barcelona.

Don Francisco had grown weary of city life, with its stifling streets and priggish manners. "A man's life must have room for adventure, Doña Pepa," he would say every time she raised an objection. "I think your brains must be drying up, Don Francisco," she would answer, teasing him with a coy smile.

The carriage, the latest landau model with thin rubber tires, was shipped ahead of the family, from Barcelona direct to Havana. Later it was transported by rail to the interior province of Camagüey, three hundred fifty kilometers east of Havana, where Don Francisco had bought a large sugar plantation for a pittance from a Spanish government official who had left the island three years earlier, during the Spanish-American war.

The Cabrera family took the more leisurely route from Barcelona to London, where Doña Pepa spent a month shopping (another concession) with their twin daughters, Isabel and Cristina, and Don Francisco used the time to explore business opportunities. Don Francisco's shadow and the apple of his eye was the Cabreras' eight-year-old son, Juan's father, Fernandito, who walked the crowded London streets beside Don Francisco, huddling under the shelter of his umbrella in the constant drizzle, and sat quietly through Don Francisco's negotiations with the English merchants.

Before they left London, Doña Pepa had six large trunks (two for herself and two for each daughter) brimming with fashionable English dresses, and Don Francisco had managed to strike a deal granting him exclusive rights to distribute the newest version of Sir Thomas Crapper's flush toilet in Havana.

From London the Cabreras sailed to New York aboard the steamship *Servia,* the sleek British liner that had the distinction of being the first all-steel passenger ship to cross the Atlantic, a distinction that pleased Don Francisco's thoroughly modern character.

After three more weeks of shopping in New York (the final concession) the Cabreras sailed to Havana on their twentieth wedding anniversary. Don Francisco engaged the ship's orchestra to play Doña Pepa's favorite tunes and they danced on the moon deck with such abandon that Doña Pepa broke the heel on one of her shoes and caused a minor scandal when she continued dancing after removing both shoes and throwing them overboard.

In Havana, Don Francisco bought a house in the exclusive El Vedado section of the city and there set up his wife and daughters, while he traveled with Fernandito to the plantation in Camagüey to build a house worthy of Doña Pepa.

Long after Don Francisco's death, up to the day of his own death, Juan's father would recall that first summer he spent in the wild "interior" of Cuba with Don Francisco as the happiest summer of his life. Juan's father never tired of telling and retelling him the stories of dove hunting with Don Francisco on the plantation that summer, toting the beautifully engraved, double-barreled shotgun Don Francisco had given him as their train pulled away from the station in Havana; stories of roasting birds over open fires on balmy evenings under the stars, of riding horses everywhere, of the nights the two spent together at the quaint little wooden hotel in the dusty town of La Esmeralda, while the country house was being built.

Juan's father would tell him these stories as Juan absent-mindedly ran his hands over the soft leather seats of the carriage while he helped his father polish the brass trim and side lanterns. The carriage had been used only once by Doña Pepa, when she tried to go to La Esmeralda to send a telegram to Havana, but it became stuck in mud three kilometers outside the main gate of the Santa Cruz, and Don Francisco had to send the overseer with a team of oxen to extract it from a bog of red clay that had threatened to swallow the carriage, the horse, the driver, and even Doña Pepa herself, who nevertheless managed to keep her composure throughout the ordeal.

After that everyone agreed that the thin, elegant wheels of the landau were not designed for the rough clay roads around the Santa Cruz, and the carriage was relegated to the northwest corner of the stables, where it sat for decades, eventually acquiring the status of a family relic.

Had life really been like this once for the Cabreras, or were these memories childhood dreams?

From the day he left the Santa Cruz at the age of seven and settled with his mother in that miserable government-assigned apartment in Havana, Juan Cabrera had begun to hide these memories, first from grief over his father's murder at the hands of the revolutionaries, and later out of fear of a world that had no place for people like the Cabreras.

Juan shut the door on his father and grandfather and invented other forebears more acceptable to the new order of things after the revolution. He became someone else, someone who was a stranger, an enemy of the Juan Cabrera who once played here.

Had he really played here, or had he dreamed it? he

wondered. And what practical difference could there be between the two now—now, when there was no one left to corroborate his memories?

Juan saw a huge ceiba tree in the distance, at the edge of the central clearing that had once comprised the farmyard and surrounding pastures of the Santa Cruz. The ceibas were sacred to the native tribes of Cuba and equally sacred to the African slaves, who called them *irokos* and firmly believed that the wrath of the gods would befall anyone who destroyed one. Sustained by twin traditions, and wrapped in a rich cocoon of mythology, the great ceibas reign over the Cuban countryside.

Juan's father had helped Don Francisco plant the ceiba that first summer they spent together in the Santa Cruz. And now the tree stood there like an ancient sentinel guarding the boundary between the clearing and the great fields of cane that spread to the foothills of the Cubitas mountain range.

Juan walked over to the ceiba tree and stood at the edge of the clearing. The sounds and fragrances of the sugarcane fields were the same sounds and fragrances he remembered from his childhood, and they evoked memories of earlier days spent playing in the yard of the great house, days filled with so much joy and such uncommon beauty that they seemed to have been made only to be lost.

By the time he returned to the central highway, the fog was coming down from the hills, cool and quiet, following the path of the streams at first, then spilling over the trees along the riverbanks and spreading like a blanket across the fields of sugarcane. Years ago, from his vantage point atop one of the framboyán trees in the Santa Cruz, the evening fog had seemed to Juan like a gentle flood as it flowed down the southern slopes of the Cubitas range, overwhelming the distant fields, gradually obliterating the cattle and horses grazing in nearby pastures, rising slowly until it covered the shacks of the sugarcane cutters and all the countryside became a broad white sea.

Chapter Two

Juan Cabrera looked down and saw that his hands were shaking, and he felt his mouth beginning to go dry again.

"Open the trunk," said the G-2 agent from State Security as he leaned his head inside the window on the driver's side. The agent did not see Juan's hands. His eyes were fixed on Raúl, who was seated behind the wheel, next to Juan.

"Open the trunk! Hurry up!"

But Raúl did not hurry. He met the agent's gaze and reached for the key in the ignition of the old, dilapidated Ford. The ignition switch was dangling halfway out of the dashboard, and the wires were showing.

Keeping his eyes on the agent's Raúl held the barrel of

the ignition switch between the two middle fingers of his right hand while he turned the key with his thumb and forefinger, taking care not to jerk on the wires. The engine dieseled for a few seconds after he pulled out the key, then it sputtered and died.

Raúl stepped out of the car and stretched to his full height, towering over the uniformed agent. The agent looked up at him, stroking the grip of his holstered pistol.

"*Vamos,* let's go, open the trunk."

Juan felt nauseous now, and he was glad the agent had not asked him to step out of the car with Raúl, because he was not sure his legs would hold him if he did. Even sitting down, he could feel the weakness in his legs, the twitching of the muscles in his thighs.

The agent followed Raúl as he walked to the back of the Ford. Two empty, dark sockets marked the place where the taillights had been. The lid of the trunk, like the rest of the car, had once been light blue. But now there were only scarce reminders of that color because the paint had worn down to the bare metal in most places and the metal had rusted over, with holes poking through here and there.

"I'll have to hold the lid up while you look. The spring is broken," Raúl said as he opened the trunk.

The agent hesitated for a moment, then glanced quickly inside the trunk and back toward Raúl. He had never seen anyone as big as Raúl, and he felt uneasy so close to the thick, muscular forearms holding up the trunk lid. The agent stepped back and looked at Raúl's broad shoulders and at his tanned, chiseled face, framed by a reddish beard.

"Where are you two headed?"

"Guanabo Beach."

"Why are you going there now?"

"Girls."

"What?"

"I just got back from Africa, from the war in Angola," said Raúl. "Do you know how long it's been since I've seen Cuban girls? Anyway, my friend knows some hot ones. At least he says they are. We're going to meet them at the beach, and drink some rum to celebrate our victory."

"What victory?"

"Our great victory against the imperialist forces in Angola. Haven't you heard? Come with us and I'll tell you all about it. Come on, *hombre,* maybe you'll get lucky with the girls at the beach."

Raúl smiled a broad, secure smile at him, and the agent saw that he was not afraid.

"Go on," the agent said harshly. "And be careful, be very careful. You're not in Angola anymore."

They had driven east from Havana on the road that winds along the north coast, through Cojímar and Alamar and Tarara. The state security agent had stopped them as they left Tarara on their way to Guanabo Beach, where Andrés was waiting with the paddles and the food and the water. They brought the three deflated inner tubes that Rogelio had sold them in Cojímar, the nylon lines, the canvas tarpaulin, and the hand-operated Czechoslovakian air pump, along with a few personal items.

"Didn't he see the stuff?" asked Juan, the color returning to his face.

"I put it under the backseat while you were inside the house talking to Rogelio," said Raúl, looking out toward the water as he cranked the engine. "It all fit nicely."

The sun was setting behind them now as they drove toward Guanabo, following the shoreline. To the east the ocean showed deep purple with shades of violet far off in the distance.

It was dark by the time they arrived at Andrés's place and drove down the narrow, winding dirt road that led to his little bungalow near the water. The road was lined with tall weeds, and Juan could see the reflection from the headlights shining on the upraised eyes of the big land crabs that came out of their burrows at night and now scurried out of the way as the car approached.

"*¡Aquí!* Over here!" called Andrés as Juan went to knock on the door of the bungalow. Andrés was returning from the water's edge, limping barefoot on the coarse sand.

"Just checking the water," he whispered with an impish smile as he came up to them.

"Well, how is it?" asked Raúl.

"Nice and warm—like bathwater."

"Let's not speak out here," said Juan.

"Yes, yes, of course, *entren,* come in, please," Andrés said, opening the door.

Inside Andrés's bungalow, a bare light bulb dangled on a black wire several feet from the ceiling at the center of the room. When the men came in, the breeze from the ocean set the bulb in motion, casting their swaying shadows on the blue walls. Three backpacks were stacked neatly in a corner next to three glass bottles filled with water. Above the bottles, three rough-hewn wooden paddles were leaning against the wall.

"Everything is ready," Andrés said as soon as they walked in.

"Have you seen any guards?" asked Juan.

"Yes, I just saw two with German shepherds down by the water."

In the harsh light from the bare bulb, Andrés looked old and frail, and Juan wondered if he was strong enough now to make the crossing. Twelve years as a political prisoner at Combinado del Este had aged him beyond his fifty-five years. His face was as wrinkled as that of a man in his eighties. Two of his teeth were missing, had got in the way of a rifle butt. And the leg they broke during the interrogation had never set right. But his spirit was fine. They never touched that. They never even came close.

And tonight Andrés was as sprightly as Juan had ever seen him. Talking about the escape, his eyes lit up like a child's on Christmas Eve. He kept saying, "I can't wait to see Margarita. I just can't wait to see Margarita."

No use trying to persuade him to stay, Juan thought.

"Have you boys eaten? Don't have much, but no reason to leave anything behind. I could heat black beans and a little rice," said Andrés.

"I'll have some," said Raúl.

"You better eat too, Juan. You'll need your strength," said Andrés.

"Do you have any rum?" Raúl asked.

"I have a bottle in the cabinet. Would you like me to pour you some?"

"No, but let me have the bottle. I'm going out to check on the guard situation while you heat the food."

Half an hour later Raúl returned, smelling of rum.

"Wouldn't take the bottle," he said.

"You didn't make them suspicious?" asked Juan.

"No. Spilled some rum on my shirt and sat there on the sand acting miserable until they found me. Told them my wife ran off with another man while I was in Angola."

"Can't believe your *cojones,*" said Juan. "You sure they didn't get suspicious?"

"Yes, I'm sure. We spoke of Africa. Showed them my medals. Told them how many imperialists I had killed and what a shock it was to get back home and find my wife gone. I think they truly felt sorry for me."

"Come on and eat before it gets cold," said Andrés.

They sat on *taburetes*—rustic wooden chairs—at a small table pushed against the wall next to the paddles, and ate the beans and rice. Raúl passed the rum around the table and each of them took a few swigs out of the bottle.

"Better wait till they move down the beach before we get the things from the car," said Juan.

"Did you get everything?" Andrés asked.

"Yes," Juan said. "But we had a close call."

"Trouble?"

"Not really," said Raúl. "Stopped around Tarara by the G-2. Young kid. Didn't look old enough to carry a gun. He was more scared than we were. Isn't that right, Juan?"

"Yes," Juan said. "He sure looked scared. Didn't see anything, either. We hid the stuff under the backseat." For a moment Juan felt ashamed to lie like that and pretend he had not been afraid. But he was used to lying by now, and soon he got over the unpleasantness and the shame.

An hour later Raúl brought the inner tubes and the air pump from the car and spread them out on the floor of the bungalow. Juan and Andrés took turns pumping air into the tubes while Raúl made trips to the car, picking up odds and ends.

"Better lash them together after we get to the beach," said Raúl. "Too awkward to take it out the door after it's put together."

"They might see us working out there," said Juan.

"Just have to take that chance," Raúl said. "In fact, don't pump them up too big here. We'll finish pumping them up at the beach. They won't get through the door if you pump them too big."

After sunset, clouds had moved in from the northwest and it was overcast and pitch black out by the water. They laid the inner tubes in a row on the coarse sand and finished pumping air into them. Every few seconds Juan stopped and looked over his shoulder. The squeaking noise the pump made each time he pushed in the rusty cylinder sounded much louder out here, and any moment he expected to see one of the guards looming over him, a growling German shepherd at his side.

They lashed the inner tubes in a straight line and strapped the tarpaulin over them. They had dragged the raft into the surf and were about to push off when Raúl decided to go back to the car.

"What the hell are you doing now?" Juan whispered.

"Just going to get a couple more lines. Be right back."

As Raúl came back with the lines, Juan saw a flashlight coming around a point off in the distance.

"Hurry, hurry, they're coming back," he whispered, on the verge of panic.

Raúl finished tying the lines, threw the paddles on the raft, and the three of them waded deeper into the water, holding on to the lashings. Soon they were drifting eastward along the coast with the outgoing tide.

By midnight the sound of barking dogs on the beach, and of an occasional passing truck, and all the other sounds of the shore that had been with them for the first few hours after they put in, had faded and died, like the glow of Havana on the horizon that had vanished behind them in the enveloping gloom.

None of them had ever been at sea. And now their eyes were fixed on the dark water, the rhythmic splashing of the paddles mesmerizing them, as they sat on the awkward raft. No one spoke. There were only the sounds of the sea.

By the time the overcast began to clear from the northwest, the paddles had grown heavy and blisters had formed on their hands. As the sea slowly turned gray with the first hint of dawn, Raúl and Andrés began to nod off.

Only Juan was still paddling when the stars above the eastern horizon dimmed with the coming sun. His eyes turned north to the rising stars of the Great Bear and then overhead to the tight Pleiades cluster, which was fading rapidly in the soft light. The wind was fair and warm and blew from the south.

A proper boat would have been easier to navigate, he thought. But a boat would have increased their chances of being detected and captured. Besides, where could they have gotten a boat? And if they had managed to find a boat, where would they have hidden it while they made their preparations and collected each item needed for the crossing? The truth is, the raft served them well. It was as fine an inner-tube raft as ever attempted the crossing.

Juan thought about the native Cubans who had lived in

the island before Columbus arrived. He remembered studying about them while he was still in elementary school, before the revolution, before everything changed. He thought about how the Tainos and the other, more primitive tribe, the Siboneys, plied these same waters in canoes dug from the trunks of their sacred ceiba trees hundreds of years before the Spanish came and discovered the green islands of the Caribbean. He remembered looking at the sea through the window in his classroom and imagining what it must have been like to kneel in a shallow dugout canoe, paddling out toward the horizon as the color of the water changed from a crystal aquamarine near the shore to a profound dark blue over the fantastic trenches and basins of the ocean floor, where steep walls drop thousands and thousands of feet to a place that is dark and cold, where the water never mixes with other, warmer waters.

Juan thought about these things and he thought about the girl with the dark hair and radiant blue eyes who was now in Miami. Then he eased his lean, muscular body into a reclining position on the canvas and fell asleep listening to the muffled sound of the water lapping against the inner tubes. He dreamed of sweet-smelling green fields of sugarcane, and his dream was so vivid that he heard the rustling of the cane in the wind and then, later in his dream, he heard the sound of hard, driving rain beating down on the tall stalks of cane.

As the morning brought the colors back to the sea, birds came from their nesting places in the river estuaries along the north coast, looking for fish. A pair of terns circled with intense concentration, one or the other occasionally diving into the warm, silky water near the raft.

Later the breeze picked up, giving the water a light chop, and dolphins began to feed on a school of mackerel north of the raft. The dolphins worked in concert, herding the mackerel into a tight circle. The mackerel churned the water inside the circle, and their frenzied movements made a sound like the rain makes when it falls on the sea. The sky was brilliant blue and broken only by a few feathery cirrus clouds moving fast to the northwest.

Two burly arms shook Juan awake. "How far have we come?" asked a groggy voice behind him.

"We came far in the night," Juan answered as he yawned. "At least twelve miles, maybe more. The outgoing tide helped."

Raúl was sitting on the inner tube lashed behind Juan's. He was leaning back now, looking at the feathery clouds. As he sat there, with his massive legs and arms and shoulders spilling over the sides of the inner tube, he looked absurd, almost comical, Juan thought.

"*Bueno,* well, I guess even if we wanted to, we couldn't go back now," said Raúl.

"Damn right," said Juan. "We beat the *contra-corriente.* We are in the main stream. We can't turn back."

The *contra-corriente* is what Cubans call the currents that spin off the Gulf Stream, like eddies, and sometimes push you back toward the coast.

Andrés was now beginning to stir.

"Who's going back?" he asked, his eyes still closed. "Are we going back?"

"Nobody's going back, Andrés," said Juan. "We're just

talking about the *contra-corriente.* We beat it last night and now we are in the great stream; we can't turn back."

"Good," said Andrés, rubbing his eyes. "I was afraid we were going back. Is anybody hungry?"

"Sure," said Raúl. "I'm starving. What have you got there?"

Andrés took out a can of Russian meat and a rusty can opener from his knapsack, which was strapped to the raft with the same line they used to secure the tarpaulin to the inner tubes. He opened the can and handed it to Raúl, saying, "Here, eat some of this. Give some to Juan, too."

"Aren't you going to have any?" Raúl asked.

"No. I'm not hungry. You and Juan eat well and finish it up."

When Juan and Raúl finished eating, Andrés untied a bottle of water that he had fastened to an eyelet on the canvas with some cord, and handed it to Raúl.

"Drink up, boys, you're going to need your strength to paddle this old man all the way to Miami!" he said, and his eyes brightened.

Andrés then reached into his knapsack and pulled out a creased clear plastic bag. The bag was folded over several times and held together with rubber bands. He removed the rubber bands and slowly unfolded the plastic. From the bag he took out a small Bible with a worn red leather cover and opened it to the place where he kept a photograph. The photograph was black and white and faded and showed a little girl about seven years old, with a big smile and cheerful dark eyes. Andrés turned the photograph over and read the name and the date scrawled in pencil on the back in a child's handwriting: *Margarita, October 29, 1967.*

He then ran his fingers over the name and remembered the day his daughter wrote it—a bright Sunday, twenty-three years ago, the day before she left for Miami. His shirt, unbuttoned to the waist, was fluttering in the light breeze. The breeze felt pleasant on his skin, and in the warmth of the morning sun, Andrés was happier than he had been in many years.

Chapter *Three*

When Juan first saw the gunboat, it was a small black dot on the southern horizon. It was a Soviet-made *Zhuk*-class fast attack boat out of the naval base at Canasí.

"I think he's coming this way," Juan said, tracking its course with his eyes.

"No, I don't think so. He can't see us," said Raúl.

"Maybe he can't see us, but he's coming this way," Juan said.

"No, he's not coming this way. It just looks that way. It's an illusion," said Raúl.

"It's no illusion. He's bearing down on us!" said Juan with such panic in his voice that he flushed, embarrassed, upon hearing himself.

"Maybe he has us on radar," Andrés said, sensing Juan's embarrassment.

"He can't have us on radar; we're too small," said Raúl.

"Maybe it's a good radar," said Juan, trying to regain his composure.

"What the hell do you know about radar?" said Raúl.

"A hell of a lot more than you! Anyway, they can probably see us already."

"No, they can't see us. It's a coincidence."

By now Juan could see the white spray where the dark bow of the gunboat split the water, and he felt his heart pounding out of control, the blood vessels pulsing in his head.

"Maybe we better lie flat," he said weakly.

"Get in the water! Everybody get in the water behind the raft! Now!" yelled Raúl.

Juan and Raúl slid into the water behind the raft. Andrés did not follow. He slowly wrapped the Bible and the photograph back in the plastic bag and replaced the rubber bands. As the twin diesels throttled down, Andrés put the bag in his knapsack and fastened the knapsack tightly to the raft.

By the time Andrés finished the last knot, he could see the pennant numbers on the gunboat and the uniformed men standing on the deck. He sat on the raft for a few more moments, unruffled, gazing at the water. Then he looked up toward the boat, waved wildly, and yelled in a deep voice, *"¡Aquí! ¡Aquí!* Here! Here!"

"What are you doing, Andrés, are you crazy?" Juan asked between his teeth, as he treaded water behind the raft.

"Quiet, they didn't see you two. They only saw me. It's the only way," Andrés whispered.

Andrés then jumped into the water and started swimming away from the raft, all the while yelling, *"¡Aquí! ¡Aquí!"*

The gunboat slowed to idle and changed its course away from the raft, toward Andrés. One of the men on the gunboat leaned over the port gunwale and started taunting him.

"Hey, worm! What are you doing in the water? Don't you know fish eat worms?" he yelled.

"What should we do with this worm?" he asked the others. "What good is a miserable, filthy worm?"

"Maybe he's good for target practice," said another.

"Yes, he'd make a good bull's-eye, wouldn't he?" the first man agreed.

As the men continued mocking Andrés, the gunboat slowly circled him, and Juan and Raúl, holding on to the raft, drifted farther away. Downwind from the boat, Juan could hear the insults and the laughter.

Andrés did not respond to the taunting. He treaded water and kept his eyes fixed on the uniformed men.

"We have to do something, Juan, the bastards might shoot him," Raúl said under his breath, his big hands squeezing the lines that held the inner tubes together.

The first man drew his pistol and aimed at Andrés's head. He then raised it a couple of degrees more and pulled the trigger.

The bullet whistled near Andrés and splashed into the water behind him. The man shot again and again, and water splashed all around Andrés. The man seemed to be a good marksman, because the bullets kept hitting the water in a small circle around Andrés's head without touching him.

Juan, hiding low in the water behind the raft, his eyes just above the surface, was peering through the narrow space between two inner tubes below the place where they were lashed together. From there he could see Andrés's arms flailing in the water and his head jerking this way and that, away from the spot where each bullet struck. Juan felt cold, as if all the blood and everything else inside his body had been squeezed out, leaving nothing there. And he began to tremble out of control.

"We've got to do something," said Raúl, squeezing the lines until they cut into the palms of his hands. "We have to get their attention before that idiot kills him."

"There's nothing we can do, Raúl, nothing. *¡Nada! ¡Nada! ¡Nada!*" said Juan, numb with terror. The word *nada* kept ringing in his head even after he stopped saying it.

It was still ringing when he saw the red and white splatter as a bullet smashed into Andrés's skull, scattering pieces of his brain on the water.

Someone on the deck of the gunboat yelled, "You've hit him!"

The boat then made a half-circle and the engines came to life, churning the water behind the stern and lifting the bow from the water.

The boat headed southeast, but Juan did not watch it go; he was staring at the dark stain made by the blood on the water where Andrés had been. It seemed small at first, but gradually spread on the surface like a cloud, growing lighter as it mixed with the sea.

When they climbed back onto the raft, the breeze was stronger and there were swells on the sea. The surface of the ocean was shimmering, and the play of the light on the water reminded Juan of the shifting patterns made by undulating fields of sugarcane on days when there was a strong wind. He tried to think about the fields and about his childhood, before everything changed. But the images of Andrés, and of his blood on the water, would not leave him.

Raúl was the first to speak.

"He did it to save us, Juan. Poor man. He said it was the only way. Didn't you hear him?"

"Yes, I heard him. I heard him say it was the only way," Juan said.

"Maybe they wouldn't have killed him if we had gotten their attention," said Raúl.

"Maybe they'd have killed us all," Juan said.

"Still, we should've done something. We should've done something, Juan."

"What could we do?"

"At least we'd have been with him."

"What good would that have done?"

"He wouldn't have been so alone," said Raúl, and tears welled in his eyes.

"He did it for us."

"Yes, he did it for us."

"He knew what he was doing."

"Yes, he knew."

Chapter *Four*

In the afternoon, flying fish began to break out of the water all around the raft, like a swarm of silver insects with stiff translucent wings rising from the sea. When they broke close to the raft, Juan could hear the rustle of their wings as they left the water, and he was surprised how far their quaint wings could carry them, always in a straight line, away from the predators that came after them from the deep.

Looking at the water, Juan tried to think about the face of the girl in Miami, but her image would not come. He tried to think of her eyes, her hair, her body, but he could not get the thought of Andrés's head out of his mind. The only thing he saw now was Andrés's head exploding, with all those clumps of brain and bone flying high in the air and then raining down, like a sudden shower splashing into the sea.

He felt responsible for the death of Andrés, and embarrassed by his own fear. Raúl would have done something if I had not stopped him, he thought. Raúl would have gotten their attention and then they would not have killed him.

But it was always like that. He would start shaking and a *negrura sofocante,* a suffocating blackness, would come over him, paralyzing him. It was as if he were not there, as if he were no longer a man. And, in truth, he was not. Then this thought would fill him with unbearable shame, and an even greater *negrura,* a profound darkness, would open up and engulf him, squeezing him, choking him. Each time this happened, he thought his life was at an end. And each time, afterwards, he wished it had ended.

Raúl sensed his distress.

"How long has it been since Carmen escaped?" he asked.

"A year," said Juan in a low voice.

"You never told me the full story," Raúl said.

"Don't know it myself. I didn't want her to talk about it when we spoke on the phone. I was afraid of losing my position teaching at the university," said Juan. "You never know who's listening."

"That's for sure," Raúl said. "Didn't she go somewhere to show off her paintings?"

"She went to an exhibition in East Berlin with people from the Ministry of Culture. Somehow she got away from them during the confusion when they tore down the wall," Juan said.

"Did you know she was going to escape?"

"No, I couldn't believe her guts when I heard," said Juan.

"Did she run into an embassy?" Raúl asked.

"She didn't tell me. I didn't want to compromise my position at the university, so I didn't let her go into it—didn't even want her to use my name when we talked. And we always used the phone at Rogelio's house," said Juan, and wondered when he had started being so afraid. Was it from the very beginning, when they took his father away, or had it come on slowly? It was hard to say. But he did not want to think about it now. He did not want to feel the *vergüenza*, the shame, that overwhelmed him whenever he thought about the things that he had done because of his fear. It was better not to think about that now.

"Who will you stay with in Miami?" he asked Raúl, pushing those thoughts out of his mind.

"My brother, I imagine," said Raúl.

"Does José Antonio know you're coming?"

"No. I never told him. I didn't want him to worry, and the last time we talked on the phone, I was still in the army—it was hard to speak openly."

"Yes, you never know who's listening."

"He was trying to get me out through Panama—always thinking of some new scheme."

"When did José Antonio leave?"

"Long time ago, before he was military age. I wouldn't know him now," said Raúl. "He's doing real well," he continued. "He owns a gas station. What about you, do you have anybody besides Carmen?"

"No. She's the only one."

"Does she know you're coming?"

"I hope so. Last time we talked, I hinted that we might try the crossing in September. Then, yesterday in Cojímar, I asked Rogelio to call her after we were gone," he said. "I also asked him to tell Carmen to call Andrés's daughter, Margarita," he added, looking down at the water.

"What are you going to do for work when you get there?" Raúl asked.

"I don't know. I expect I'll just get whatever job I can at first, then see what happens. But I hope to teach physics and astronomy again at some university. My English is good, and I packed my diplomas and certificates," said Juan. "What will you do?"

"I guess I'll go to work for my brother. He's thinking of buying another gas station."

"Maybe he'll put you in charge of it."

"Yes. Maybe he will."

"Are you hungry?"

"No. I don't feel like eating. Do you?"

"No."

At sunset, the high, feathery clouds that had been coming in bands from the southeast all day turned delicate shades of pink and purple, but they kept their plume shape and did not change their speed or direction.

The current felt stronger now and carried them steadily toward the northeast. The speed of the wind decreased after sunset and came only in weak gusts. But Juan thought the swells seemed greater in the dying light, and the raft rose and fell with the sea.

Juan turned his eyes to the west and looked at a group of stars that were beginning to flicker dimly near the horizon. He knew the constellation well. It was Boötes, the

Herdsman. He then looked for other familiar stars and got his bearings. Since he was a boy he had loved to study the heavens. It was one of the few constant things, one of the few comforts in his life. And the perfect regularity of the constellations, each one always at its appointed place in its own season, was the only thing now that reminded him of his childhood.

He showed Raúl the dim North Star, Polaris, dangling at the end of the tail of the Little Bear, and they paddled toward it as best they could, riding the rising swells.

Later the air grew cooler and a heavy fog enveloped them. Juan lost sight of the stars, and he was not sure they hadn't turned around, going over one of the swells. So they decided it would be more prudent to stop paddling and just drift with the current.

Toward the end of the night, after Raúl was asleep, Juan felt something big and heavy bump the inner tubes. It frightened him, and to allay his fear, he tried to imagine it was a passing dolphin, playing with the raft. But the bump came again; then he felt it through the inner tubes, long and sleek, slipping under the raft, and he never heard blowing sounds.

The morning was gray, and there was a soft mist over the water. On the southern horizon there were towering build-ups of purple cumulus clouds. Juan felt cold. The moist air raised goosebumps on his skin, which was already sore in places from the sun and the salt water.

Raúl took out a can of condensed milk and some crackers wrapped in a plastic bag and shared them with him. They dipped the crackers into the can and scooped up globs of the thick, sweet milk.

Late in the morning, Juan saw the disk of the sun for the first time that day. It was obscured by a thin veil of clouds and he could look at it without hurting his eyes, as if through a smoked lens filter. But after a while the sun disappeared behind a thick overcast, and he did not see it again until just before sunset. The rain came in spurts throughout the day, and the moving squalls concealed the horizon.

"I haven't been this wet since I was in Africa," said Raúl. "Remember Pepito García, the one we called Orejas, 'Ears'?"

"Yes, I remember him. Didn't he play third base on our team?" asked Juan.

"Yes. Yes, he did. Anyway, he was killed in Angola, near Matale," said Raúl. "We were on patrol, making our way through the underbrush. It had been raining all day and we were drenched. Pepito was out front when the ambush came. Part of his right leg was blown off by a mortar shell."

"Was he killed instantly?" Juan asked, feeling that strange combination of guilt, embarrassment, and curiosity that men who have not been in combat feel when they speak about war with men who have.

"No, he died on the way. I carried him back to the base on my shoulders. He was such a little guy, hardly weighed anything. He kept telling me to put him down and leave him there. He was worried about me; he thought he was slowing me down. But of course he really wasn't slowing me down at all because he was such a little guy, didn't weigh a thing. He didn't cry or complain about the pain, not even once," Raúl said. "The worst part is they never brought him home, never brought him back to his family. They just opened a hole and dumped him in it, like he was garbage."

"They never brought anybody home," he continued. "Not Pepito, not Armando—El Flaco, the skinny one—nobody. And for what? I'll tell you for what," said Raúl, answering his own question. "For *nada,* for *mierda.*"

The wind was fitful and strange through the afternoon. It came in sudden, powerful gusts that raised fine spray from the crests of the swells, and then died as quickly as they came. Once, during a gust, a flying fish struck Juan on his back and fell behind him on the raft. He turned around and watched it for a moment, its wings quivering on the canvas. Then he saw Raúl pick it up, his large hands gently avoiding the wings, and place it back into the sea.

At sunset the overcast began to break. Juan looked at a clear patch of sky that was now a haunting shade of luminous blue that sometimes shows between dark clouds toward the end of a September afternoon. Through the opening he could see the same delicate, plume-shaped clouds they had seen in the morning, still racing to the northwest, dressed in the soft pastels of the evening.

In the twilight, great flocks of terns appeared from the south, flying low over the water. They passed over the raft in endless waves and filled the air with their strange mournful cries. Juan and Raúl watched each wave as it vanished over the northern horizon, only to be replaced by another and yet another noisy wave of countless little dark birds.

Chapter *Five*

The ancient tribes that lived in Cuba before the Spaniards had a name for the spirit that uprooted the great ceiba trees in their verdant forests, demolished their thatch-roofed huts, and devastated their crops. Days before the spirit arrived, their wise men, the *behiques,* could see the signs of his coming in the shape of the clouds and in the waves of the sea.

When the *behiques* uttered his name, the native Cubans left their villages in the coastal plains and fled to the purple hills, carrying their children. There they sought refuge in the caves and cowered in terror until the awesome roar of his fury passed.

The Spanish conquerors paid no heed to the legends of the native Cubans. They enslaved the island tribes and forced them to mine gold. Those who would not yield to their yoke, like the proud Siboneys, were slaughtered. Finding little gold in the islands, the Spaniards moved on and pillaged the gold of the tribes on the mainland. Every year, great fleets laden with treasure gathered at the port of Havana and took on provisions before starting their passage back to Spain across the Atlantic, protected by powerful war galleons.

Sometimes, after the ships' lookouts lost sight of the fort of El Morro guarding the entrance to the harbor, the wind would rise over the warm waters of the Gulf Stream and dark clouds would envelop the ships. Giant foamy waves would wash over the planked decks, and the massive masts of Spanish oak would snap like matchsticks. The timbers would creak and strain with the violence of the sea. And, just before the hulls tore open and disgorged them into the black water, the Spaniards would be haunted by the sound of the name they had heard only in whispers from the lips of their slaves while they loaded the ships, the fearsome name of Huracán, the spirit that brought the big wind.

Four centuries later, on the night that Juan and Raúl met Andrés in the darkness of Guanabo Beach, this same primeval force was beginning to stir, once more, over the balmy waters of the Caribbean.

As they pumped air into the inner tubes spread on the sand, nine hundred miles away a heavy, steady rain was falling on the sea south of Jamaica. The air, warmed by the tropic sea, began to rise, slowly at first, into the jumbled mass of rain clouds.

North of them, at the National Hurricane Center in Coral Gables, Florida, expert eyes studied satellite photographs, and a weather reconnaissance airplane, bristling with exotic instruments, had just left the runway and was banking south over the brightly lit skyline of Miami.

Reports from ships in the central Caribbean, warning of rising winds and swelling seas, poured into the Hurricane Center throughout the night. By the morning of the first day the three of them were at sea, the probing aircraft had confirmed cyclonic wind circulation and exceedingly low air pressure at the center. The latest satellite photographs now clearly showed the eye, a circular area of eerie calm and light at the center of the whirling wind. The storm, driven by steering currents of air, moved north and gathered strength from the nurturing water.

Late on the night of the first day, violent gales tore through the forests of western Jamaica, ripping up trees in their path. Ugly, oozing walls of mud, loosened by torrential rains, came down the hills, burying cars and sweeping away shacks on the outskirts of Montego Bay.

Jamaica presented little hindrance to the passage of the winds. Leaving the devastated island behind, the hurricane quickly regained its fury and moved on inexorably toward the southern coast of Cuba.

The seabirds that make their nests in the mangroves covering the cays and islets south of Cuba had left long before the sea started to rise. Something in them sensed the coming storm. In the coastal swamps, bullfrogs buried themselves deep in the mud, and farther north, in the rolling pastures of central Cuba, cattle huddled close together on the lee side of hills.

Early in the afternoon of the second day, the hurricane skirted the colonial town of Trinidad, lying in a coastal plain that extends between the dark green, curvaceous mountain range called Escambray and the blue Caribbean. The storm surge flooded the beach communities and pushed the raging sea deep into the sweet, clear waters of the Manatí River, which spilled beyond its banks and inundated the fertile flood plain.

It then moved westward along the coast and turned sharply to the north at the Bay of Cienfuegos. Soviet warships lying at anchor in the protected waters of the harbor strained at their massive anchor chains as they swung ponderously, like giant weathercocks, to face the screaming wind.

The great whirlwind passed over the harbor, lifting and tossing small boats, like toys, over seawalls and onto the streets and alleys of the city. Violent, wind-driven rains battered the lush sugarcane fields as the hurricane cut a path of destruction across the center of the island on its way toward the north coast of Cuba and the Straits of Florida.

Over the Straits, the stars covered the night in a vast, shining blanket. The air was crisp and the wind came stronger now. It felt cool on Juan's skin as it blew them to the northwest across the Gulf Stream. In the darkness, a few stragglers from the flocks of terns flew over the raft. Juan could not see them, but he heard their small, sad voices calling the others, and then, later in the night, he heard no more birds.

Deep below them, in the silent blackness, giant marlin swam eastward with the current, chasing schools of ballyhoo toward the Great Bahama Bank. To the north, in the backcountry of Florida Bay, between the Everglades and the Florida Keys, bonefish and permit were on a feeding frenzy, churning the shallow littoral waters.

Juan lay on his back, resting on the wet canvas, staring blankly at the sky, turning his head every once in a while to look at Raúl. In the starlight, Raúl's face looked as pale as marble, and the wind blew his disheveled hair, giving him a ghostly appearance.

Near dawn, after thick, rolling clouds spread across the sky, Juan drifted into an uneasy and fitful sleep. He dreamed Andrés was calling him from a dark beach. He could hear the sound of dry palm fronds shaken by a stiff wind blowing over the desolate sand. Then he heard Andrés's deep voice rise above the howling wind and call his name from the shore. The voice had the mellow tone of an old mission bell, as it rose above the wind and called out to Juan, asking him to wait: *"¡Espera, Juan! ¡Por favor, espera!"*

Juan awoke with a start and felt confused. Later, in his half-slumber, the voice returned. This time it was calling him from the sea, and he heard the sound of desperate thrashing on the water. Then Juan dreamed he saw Andrés's hand reach out to him from the dark water next to the raft. He tried to grasp it before it sank back into the sea, but he could not move; his fear would not let him move. He wanted to scream, to ask Raúl for help. But there was no sound when he opened his mouth. It was as if he were not there at all, as if he did not exist: unable to move, unable to talk, everything in him paralyzed by his profound terror. And he saw Andrés's hand, with the fingers outstretched, sink silently and vanish into the black, fathomless water.

Chapter *Six*

Hard rain stung Juan's face. He opened his eyes and saw tumbling masses of clouds racing above him in the half-light of dawn. Solid gray curtains of rain came toward them from the southeast. As each curtain arrived over the raft, it enclosed them in a watery cocoon, cutting them off from the rest of the world. Cataracts of water poured on them, drenching their supplies.

During one of the downpours, Raúl unfastened the bottle of water next to him and began to collect rainwater by wringing his soaked shirt into the bottle. He held the bottle between his legs and tried to keep his balance as the raft rode the rising sea. Before he could replace the cap on the bottle, a sudden gust of wind lifted the raft into the air and Juan saw the bottle Raúl was holding fly away from him, tumbling madly, like an odd glass projectile shot from an invisible cannon. Raúl grabbed one of the lines with his left hand and wrapped his right arm around Juan's waist as Juan tumbled backwards out of the raft.

The blast pushed the raft across the water and they dragged behind it as if towed by a frenzied sea monster. Raúl clutched Juan tightly in one arm and held the raft with the other while they crashed through raging, gray-white walls of water. The spray choked and blinded Juan and turned his world into a gray, deafening roar. Salt water hit his face with such unrelenting violence that he felt as though his eyes were being wrenched out of their sockets. It pushed into his nose and ran down his throat, stinging and burning his throat and sinuses.

The next moment they were airborne again, somersaulting through space and slamming into the side of a slate-colored, mountainous swell. In the rolling confusion of the crash, Raúl managed to pin Juan between himself and the raft and grab another line with his right hand. Juan then groped blindly for the lashings between the inner tubes, found them, and held on, at the same time wrapping his legs around one of the tubes.

The raft was now in a deep, dark trough between the towering swells, and the wind spun it like a grotesque merry-go-round. White, shroudlike sheets of airborne foam hid the world above them.

Juan felt strange to be dying with no one to mourn him except Carmen. He wondered if it would have felt different with children to leave behind. Is it more natural for people with children, he thought, or does everyone feel equally strange at the last moment, when there is no doubt that it is the last moment; or, he thought, is there always a doubt? Will I doubt even when the salt water fills my lungs, or will I say to myself then, *Now. The time is now; there will never be another time like this; there will never be another time at all . . . and I will never be again.* He was amazed at the strangeness and he was amazed at his own thoughts.

Juan's reverie ended when the crest of a huge wave collapsed upon them in a watery explosion. The force of the water pushed the raft ten feet under the surface and he found himself submerged, face upward, looking at a surreal cloud of minute bubbles rising slowly away from his face toward the surface of the sea.

He then felt himself tugged upward and was surprised to find his left hand still grasping one of the lines, without the least awareness of willfully doing it. In the dim, murky light he caught a blurry glimpse of his fingers wrapped around the line, and he felt as though he were looking at the severed claw of a crab that continues to grapple its prey even after it is wrenched from the body of the animal. He saw the line was looped around his wrist, and as he followed the raft to the surface, he wound a couple more loops with a quick motion of his arm.

His head broke the surface and he gasped and gagged as he swallowed a foamy mixture of air and brine. Juan then peered into the blowing mist, looking for Raúl, his eyes burning with salt water, and did not see him. He called out his name, but the wind overpowered his voice and he only heard the sound of the wind, which blew so strongly now that it flattened the tops of the waves.

Toward the end of the third night, the hurricane left the north coast of Cuba through the Bay of Cardenas, crossed the harbor, and cut across the thin peninsula of Hicacos, which forms the north rim of the bay and separates its waters from the much deeper waters of the Straits. It moved in the darkness over the Gulf Stream and came upon them west of the Cay Sal Bank, a triangular area of shoals, rocks and shallows lying between the north coast of Cuba and the Florida Keys.

The hurricane hit them head-on, fifty miles west of Elbow Cay, a tiny, slender spit of coral rocks and sand at the westernmost edge of the Cay Sal Bank. The sun was rising as the leading edge of the spinning winds struck the raft, but they could not see it. The outer gales blew them westward, against the Stream, toward the Gulf of Mexico, and the clouds concealed them from the bright colors of the morning and held them in a private darkness.

The strongest winds, the inner ones, raced around the eye in a tight counterclockwise circle and leveled the heads of the waves below them. But inside the eye itself, where the wind was calm, there were strange, fluttering, cone-shaped waves that seemed confused and moved in different directions, tumbling and crashing into each other.

The sound of the wind, which had been a deep, thundering roar to this point, grew shriller as the eye approached. The innermost gusts blew the raft sideways over the water, as the breeze blows a leaf across a pond.

Juan's only care now was getting air into his lungs as he held the line and dragged behind the raft with his face in the water. Like a swimmer in a race, he brought his face out of the water every few seconds with a quick rotating motion and took a quick gasp of air. He was grasping one of the two nylon ropes that Raúl had tied to the inner tube at either end of the raft, while the three of them carried the raft into the surf at Guanabo Beach.

Juan remembered wading into the warm water of Guanabo, coarse grains of sand between his toes, his heart pounding and his ears cocked, expecting at any time to hear the sound of heavy boots trampling the crisp, dry sea grape leaves strewn along the sand. And he thought about the hard time that he and Andrés had given Raúl as he tied the two eight-foot lengths of rope that he had brought back from the car at the last minute. He remembered whispering, between clenched teeth, "Dammit, Raúl, hurry up! Why are you wasting time with those stupid ropes?"

Andrés was much calmer and kidded Raúl in a good-natured way, "What are those lines for, Raúl, are we going to be docking somewhere?"

Even though that was only three days ago, it seemed that it was in another lifetime now, as Juan clung to the thin nylon line that kept him in this world.

At the threshold between the innermost gales and the eye of the hurricane—that improbably thin horizon that separates the Armageddon of all winds from perfect calm—arises a monstrous wave. It is the origin of all the waves that radiate out from the hurricane and travel hundreds of miles across the ocean, heralding, under brilliant skies and pleasant breezes, the coming wind.

This wave, crowned by purple-black clouds, now arose from the sea behind the raft like the mountainous back of a great behemoth. Juan could not see it approaching, but he sensed the change in the sea as he began to rise toward the peak of the giant swell.

The scale of the wave was so out of proportion to his own

puny dimensions that it seemed to Juan that the whole of the sea was rising below him, thrusting him higher and higher and higher, through the swirling madness of clouds, like an offering to the god of the wind.

When he reached the peak of the rising water, Juan felt in the pit of his stomach that lurching, weightless feeling that comes at the top of a roller-coaster ride. The raft teetered atop the crest for a moment before the uppermost eddies cast it over the rim and down the sheer back of the wave. The raft cut a tiny furrow in the smooth, dark green wall of the swell as it came down, almost vertically, toward the trough dug by the wind at the base. In the splashing chaos, Juan felt a heavy bulk bump against his chest. At the same time, a pair of powerful arms clasped him in a bear hug. *¡Raúl! ¡Dios mio! My God!* He must have held to the other line, Juan thought, as they clung to each other flipping through the air.

The water and the sky and the foam and parts of thoughts—of Carmen, of her eyes, of waiting for his father amid the fields of sugarcane—swirled in Juan's mind as he plunged into the sea.

The sun was shining when he returned to the surface. The color of the sky was a soft powdery blue, and it was clear except for some wispy white clouds that seemed to be materializing over him. These clouds looked delicate and were exquisitely formed, as if each line were painted with a very fine brush, and they had the elegant shape of the tailfeathers of a rooster. The wind had died, and everywhere there were birds that flew in circles around them and filled the sky with their plaintive cries. There were small, dark terns with snowy breasts and many kinds of sea gulls and large, ungainly pelicans diving into the sea in sudden splashes, their wings never fully retracting before striking the water. There were even some land birds, and these looked lost and out of place as they circled, confused and exhausted, searching for a place to perch in this unsubstantial, fluid universe of sea and sky, where the single reality was transformation and where there was not so much as the slimmest twig to be grasped and held, solidly and comfortably, with a claw.

Twenty yards north of them, what remained of the raft was bobbing on the water. There were small blue birds huddling close together and covering every bit of exposed surface on the raft. The tarpaulin was in tatters, and they could see a few ragged strips of canvas floating on the water, still attached to the inner tubes by the lines tied to the eyelets.

They swam toward the raft, jostled on their way by peculiar conical waves that seemed to rise and fall around them without traveling much distance on the horizontal plane, as proper waves normally do.

With great effort they pulled themselves onto the inner tubes, scaring away the tired, swallowlike birds, which then circled above them until a few brave ones alighted on their backs as the two of them lay facedown, exhausted, on top of the raft.

When Juan looked up, the scene that unfolded before him was of a haunting and terrible beauty unlike anything he had ever experienced or even imagined before. Raúl kept whispering, "*El ojo, el ojo,* the eye, the eye," like an obscure religious incantation. Juan kept silent as he looked around, eyes wide open, taking in what few men have seen in this world.

They were now at the center of an immense bowl carved out of a mass of dark clouds. The wall of clouds completely encircled them, sloping steeply away as it rose toward heaven in all directions, forming terraces like tiers in a colossal stadium. Above the perfectly smooth rim at the top of the wall, the brilliant tropical sun was shining in regal splendor. The color of the sea was a deep emerald green, and all around the base of the clouds there was a wall of white water, as if someone had taken all the waterfalls in the world and arranged them in a circle, fifteen miles in diameter. And in the distance, from all directions at once, Juan could hear the deep roar of the water and the higher, more ominous sound of the wind.

"We're in the eye," said Juan.

"I know. The worst is yet to come."

"How long do you think we have before the wind picks up again?"

"Twenty minutes . . . maybe less."

"You think we can ride it out?"

"Don't know," said Raúl in a low voice. Then he added, "Maybe," his voice rising and sounding more hopeful. "We've made it this far."

"Even if we make it, how are we going to survive afterwards with everything gone?" Juan asked.

"Don't know."

"Everything gone! The water, the food . . . everything!"

"Yes, even my cigar," said Raúl.

"You packed a cigar?"

"Yes."

"Why in the world would you pack a cigar?"

"Why not? I figured I'd save it till we arrived. Then I'd strut up on the beach, pull out my cigar, and light it."

"You're crazy, Raúl. You're completely crazy!"

"I know. I'm here with you, aren't I?"

"We better get ready."

"Yes."

A line had cut into one of the three inner tubes and deflated it. They still had two good ones, though. To avoid another mishap, Raúl pulled his pocket knife from a zippered pocket in his army trousers and cut two wide strips of rubber from the bad one, and they used these strips to reinforce the area around the two good inner tubes where they wrapped fresh lines, fastening them with square knots.

"How's your side coming?" Raúl asked.

"Good," Juan replied.

"Make sure the knots are strong, and tie a few extra ones for more security."

"They say the winds behind the eye are the worst."

"Yes. I've heard that."

"Maybe it just seems worse because the strongest winds hit you first, instead of building up gradually as they did with the leading edge," Juan said.

"That's good."

"Why?"

"Because if we make it through the first part, we'll know we're okay. We'll know it's behind us instead of the other way round."

"I hope you're right."

"But, whatever happens, we better stay in the water until it is all over and just let the inner tubes drag us along like they did before."

"Yes, that seems to work."

"If we climb on top too early, before it is truly over, a sudden gust might flip us."

"Yes, we'll stay in the water and put as little strain on the raft as possible."

"The secret is to stay low."

"We can't get any lower."

"I hope not."

Juan's wrists and the palms of his hands had been cut by the ropes during the first part of the storm, and were bleeding now in the water as he worked tying the lines, but he did not feel the pain. He tied a loop around the far end of each line to slip around his wrists. Before tightening the loop, he used Raúl's knife to cut two small strips of rubber from the deflated inner tube and wrapped them around his wrists for protection.

The roar grew louder, and as he worked securing the lines, Juan looked back over his shoulder every few minutes to check the progress of the approaching wall, which loomed over them now, casting its shadow on the sea. He saw the shadow pass over them and race ahead to the north, darkening the water as it passed.

"Ready?" Raúl asked.

Juan was holding his line with a distant look and did not answer.

"Make sure they're good and tight," Raúl added.

"Listen, if I don't make it, tell Carmen—"

"You'll make it."

A greater darkness came now as a low, gray mantle of clouds spread over the water. A heavy mist surrounded the raft moments before the sea broke over them and the wind began to flail them. The wind now came from the opposite direction and blew them with the current to the northeast, toward the Florida Keys, as the great storm straddled the Straits.

With the rolling countryside of Cuba behind it, the hurricane was now once more in its element as it drew its life from the Gulf Stream. The current gave its warmth to the wind, and as the hurricane drained energy from the water, it left in its wake a cold trail on the surface of the sea. Viewed from space, one set of spiraling arms could be seen racing over the southern tip of the Everglades, bringing showers to that fragile, broad river of grass while, at the same time, another set of arms was still pouring rain over the northernmost Cuban cities, including Havana.

In Miami, grocery store shelves had been emptied by excited housewives who, in their enthusiasm to make sure their families were prepared, had bought more food and supplies than they could possibly consume in a month's time. Radio stations blared the latest coordinates in English and Spanish, and the Overseas Highway, stretching more than one hundred miles from Key West to the mainland, was jammed with cars inching their way north. At Dinner Key Marina, as in scores of other marinas dotting the bays and inlets of south Florida, boatmen were securing their yachts, lashing rows of old automobile tires to the lifelines and hanging them over the sides to protect the gunwales, reminding themselves to leave plenty of slack in the mooring lines to allow for the rising sea.

From a studio window atop a high-rise on Brickell Avenue, a brunette with violet eyes was watching the whitecaps on Biscayne Bay. As she looked south across the water, she held a telephone to her ear waiting for her friend at the Coast Guard base to pick up on the other end.

"Hello, Vivian? Carmen. Anything?"

"No. No one has been picked up today."

"Will the hurricane keep them in port?"

"No. The cutters are out, and they'll stay at sea until the storm passes. We've deployed them to the east, out of the way, so they'll be ready to swing south and come in behind the hurricane."

"Any idea where it will hit?"

"It's headed straight toward Key West right now. Did you get through to Juan?"

"No, the lines are down."

"I'm sure he's all right. Radio Martí put out advisories early on. He's probably at home right now, trying to get through to you."

"Please, Vivian, let me know the minute you hear they've picked up anybody."

"Don't worry, you'll be the first to know."

"Thanks. By the way, I finished your son's portrait. If you swing by my apartment tonight, I'll have it for you."

"I think I'll wait till the hurricane passes."

"Any chance it will hit Miami?"

"Probably not. After Key West, it's predicted to cross Florida Bay and make landfall somewhere between Sanibel and Tampa. But anything can happen. I'll be at the base until it passes, in any event."

"I'm glad. I feel better knowing you're there. Let me know if I can help in any way."

"Thanks."

Chapter

Seven

The colors of the sky grew softer after sunset. A few trailing cloud ribbons flushed pink as they raced northward over the western horizon. Above these flat, tenuous clouds, a thin crescent moon was beginning to glimmer in the fading light, and a gentle breeze blew over the water.

Juan and Raúl were shivering as they pulled themselves up on the raft. They lay on their backs, shaking violently, with their arms folded across their chests.

"Juan, are we still in the Stream?"

"Yes, we have to be."

"Why does the water feel so cold?"

"Don't know. Maybe the hurricane drew the heat from the sea."

"You think it blew us into the Gulf?" Raúl asked.

"No, the trailing edge blew us to the northeast, so we should be closer to the Keys."

"Are you sure?"

"Yes. Why are you so worried? It's not like you to be worried."

"Just had a bad feeling all of a sudden."

"Like what?"

"I felt I was never going to see land again."

"But the worst is over, Raúl. We made it through."

"I know, it was just a strange feeling."

"You're just hungry. That's what Andrés would have said."

"I must be. I'm beginning to think weird thoughts, like I always do when I get hungry. But it sure was strong."

"What was strong?"

"The fee . . . Never mind, I'm just hungry. That's all. I'm hungry as hell."

Along with everything else, the storm had taken the three paddles Andrés had carved from a single twelve-foot length of pine board. The loss of the paddles bothered Raúl even more than the loss of the food and the water. Raúl was a practical, physical man, at ease in the everyday world of objects. No matter how remote or bleak the place, or how dismal the circumstances, he always found structure and meaning in his universe as long as he held a machete or a shovel or an ax or any other tool securely in his hands. The very *act* of digging a trench or cutting a path through the jungle brought him comfort.

Even though, like Juan, he was a stranger to the sea, Raúl made himself at home in this new world and, paddle in hand, attacked the waves as he had, at other times in distant places, conquered the jungle with his machete and broken the earth with his shovel.

Unlike Juan, who had taught physics and astronomy at the University of Havana, Raúl was not comfortable in the ethereal world of ideas. He was, without pretension, a *guajiro,* a man of the earth, and he distrusted those things he could not touch and hold in his hands. How can a man, without ever touching it, weigh and measure a star? Raúl could not understand it, and he did not completely believe it.

Now, adrift, without anything to do and without a tool to do anything, Raúl felt, for the first time in his life, truly lost. His soul was restless as disturbing thoughts raced through his mind. He felt resentment toward Juan, who, never having been at sea, spoke with assurance about the speed and direction of the currents; who always pointed the way they should go, day or night; who could barely tie a decent knot, but who regularly announced their location on the black, trackless water by measuring the height of the North Star, stretching out his arm and aligning the bottom of his closed fist with the horizon. A closed fist was ten degrees, *he* said. A finger's width was two-point-five degrees, *he* said. Now they were twenty-four degrees north latitude, better than halfway there, *he* said. Why should he believe Juan, who, after all, was a damned liar and a coward? No, he didn't even want to *think* about that, or about the things Juan had done, not now.

Raúl resented Juan and his knowledge acquired from books, and he resented his own reliance on that knowledge.

"Juan, are you *sure* we didn't get blown into the Gulf of Mexico?"

"Yes, I'm sure."

"Why?"

"We were too far to the east by the time it hit us, and the tail end must have blown us closer to the Keys."

"How far do you think we are?"

"Around forty miles south of Key West."

In the dark water, they saw bright green phosphorescent streaks as unseen fish darted, like meteors, under the inner tubes. Pangs of hunger gnawed at Raúl, and he thought about the tasty fish swimming beneath them and he imagined that he was frying them now on a big cast-iron frying pan over the open flame of a campfire under the stars. He could smell the onions and the green peppers and he could hear the pan sizzle as he squeezed lime juice, plenty of lime juice, over the delicious blackened fillets, and his mouth watered.

"Do you think we might be able to catch a fish?" he asked Juan.

"How?"

"Don't know, just thought you might have an idea."

After midnight, Juan saw the constellation of Orion rise majestically in the east and he showed it to Raúl. Then he lay on his back, looking at the stars until he fell asleep.

He dreamt that Orion the hunter, the son of Neptune, was walking on the sea, as he used to do before he was killed. In his dream, the good giant Orion came walking sadly on the surface of the sea and passed him in the darkness and did not see him but walked on by, without disturbing the waves, and disappeared forever in the west amid a crowd of stars.

The morning was bright and calm. Great patches of yellow sargasso weed covered the sea around the raft. Tiny crabs and shrimp crawled around the little air sacs that kept the seaweed afloat. Sleek blue and gold dorados swam in the shade under the seaweed, waiting for the smaller fish that fed on the miniature crustaceans.

Raúl picked up a clump and saw the colorful half-inch crabs scurrying around the thickly matted branches. He reached in, searching with his fingers, and pulled one out. He held it between his thumb and forefinger as the tiny pincers opened and closed grasping the air. He threw it into his mouth, cracking the salty shell between his molars. It tasted better than he thought it would. He tried another and then another, chewing them and letting the juices run over his tongue.

"These taste good, Juan. Here, try one."

Juan chewed a crab and then tried one of the shrimp. They *are* tasty, he thought. It had not occurred to him that they would taste this good uncooked.

Raúl's spirit was lifted by his discovery, and he began to think how he might catch one of the dorados swimming under the inner tubes. The shrimp and crabs were good, but they were not sufficient. If he could only figure out a way to capture a big dorado, they would eat well, very well, he thought. Then their only problem would be fresh water, and he had already thought of a way to collect rainwater, using the remnants of the deflated inner tube. All he needed was rain, and it was bound to rain. Of course it would rain. It always rains, he thought.

An idea then began to form in his mind about how he would capture a dorado. He reached into the water and undid the two eight-foot lines he had lashed to the raft at Guanabo. He took the end of one line and made a big S. He then took the end of the other line and tied it across the top curve of the S to make an enclosure. He continued making S's with the first line and tying the second one straight across, and then, after a while, he came back, tying knots along the center part of the S's, and made a number of rows like that until he began to see something that looked like a net.

When he first started thinking about his idea, he thought he would have to cut the lines in many places, and that it would be laborious and take a long time. Thinking about that, he reached down and felt around the zippered pocket of his army trousers for his pocket knife and confirmed it still was safely tucked in there. But as he began to work with the lines, he realized that he hardly had to cut them at all, and that it was easier than he thought it would be. But when he had used up the lines, he saw that the size was not adequate, and he was surprised at how small a net sixteen feet of line made. He then noticed that the quarter-inch nylon rope he was using was actually made of four separate smaller strands twined together. He undid what he had done, unraveled the individual strands, and repeated the process using the smaller strands. He also took the lashings that had held the remnants of the deflated inner tube to the other two and used them to get more strands. He saved the rubber remnants to make a container for rainwater; he would figure out the exact details for that project later.

In a few hours, after several attempts using different

knots and approaches, he had what looked like a decent net, about four feet by four feet when he stretched it out. The problem now was to wait for a dorado to come swimming under his inner tube and trap it in the net. He did not expect immediate success—that was not his nature, and he had lived long enough to know that success was hardly ever immediate. Sometimes it was, but that was luck, and he did not trust luck. He did trust his perseverance and he knew he had plenty of that in reserve. But he was not sure exactly how he would go about capturing his dorado. He figured he would try the first thing that came to mind, and if that didn't work, he would keep modifying his technique until he found one that did. It is not important to know exactly how to do something, he thought. It is only important to know that you are going to do it. And he knew he was going to catch his dorado or—at worst—another fish that was not so fast. But he hoped it would be a big, tasty dorado.

The sun was high, and shone down into the water that was now a deep dark blue. The hurricane had churned the water and made it look greenish and strange as it passed. But the powerful currents of the Gulf Stream had swept all that water away during the night, and now it was blue again and warm like before. The rays of the sun penetrated deep into the water, and the men could clearly see the different fish as they swam by under the raft.

Raúl lay on his stomach across the inner tube, with his head and upper body hanging over the side. He gathered two corners and the middle of one side of the net and held them with his teeth, making a sort of scoop. He then held the two remaining corners in his hands and stretched his long arms as far as he could under the raft. As soon as he did that, he thought that he should have gathered some of those little shrimp and crabs and dropped them under the raft to attract smaller fish that would then get the attention of the dorados. It was too late now, though. He had gone to some trouble getting one end of the net just right in his mouth to make a scoop, and now he was in this awkward position and he decided to wait and see if it worked before he tried anything else.

After a while he saw a greenish golden shape rise from the deep and approach the raft, sparkling as it moved in the sunlight. Then it came under the raft and hung suspended in the shade. It was a male dorado, about ten pounds. With his eyes close to the water, Raúl could see the fish as it inspected the underside of the raft. He could see it gradually adjust its position, slowly moving its pectoral fins. Then he saw it as it began to bump the bottom of his inner tube with its prominent forehead. The magnificent colors of the living dorado amazed Raúl. He had seen dorado before, but always at the docks, as fishermen flung the dead fish on the rough concrete. Even there, stiff and lifeless, and stripped of all dignity, they were beautiful fish. He could tell the males from the females by their high foreheads, tapering back to the forked, swallowlike tails. But he had always thought their color in life was the same dull gray they displayed in death, and when he was a boy, he wondered, without ever bothering to ask anyone, why the fishermen called them *dorados,* which in Spanish means "golden ones." He had later decided that the name probably had more to do with the spirit of the fish than with its true color, since he had heard fishermen describe them as great fighters. But after a while he grew up and stopped wondering about this and other inconsistencies.

Now, as he watched the fish in the full splendor of life, he could see the deep blue of its back, which started out at the top almost purple, like the Gulf Stream. As the blue came down its sides, he noticed how it gradually grew lighter and lighter until it began to blend with the gold along the middle. The mixture of the blue and the gold produced an exuberance of greens from deep emerald to the most delicate color of the freshest spring. Then the green, farther down, yielded to the gold, which, like the blue, started out in deep hues. At first it was like tarnished brass, with dark spots. Then it descended through all the possible shades of gold so that the belly of the fish looked almost silver. But even there, at the very bottom, there were specks of gold. And, as the fish turned in a shaft of light, all of those colors, all of them at once, exploded in a fantastic burst of brilliant tones of gold. Seeing that, Raúl remembered the stiff, dull bodies on the dock and he knew what no one who is a prisoner of the shore would ever know. He knew why the fishermen of his boyhood called them dorados, the golden ones, and why the name had such a sad and distant sound whenever they pronounced it.

Raúl lay still now, with his outstretched arms in the water, and held his breath as the dorado edged closer and closer to the suspended net. The water magnified the fish like a lens, and it looked huge to him as it poked its head over the open end of the net. He could hear his heart beating so loudly that he was afraid it would scare away the fish, and he could feel the pounding of his blood inside his head. Raúl waited until the entire fish was over the net, and then raised his arms against the inner tube and brought them together in one quick motion.

The upper half of his trunk was already hanging over the side, and this movement was so violent and sudden that he plunged headfirst into the sea, grasping the net under the water and thrashing the surface with his feet. In the blurry, bubbling confusion he saw a quick flash as the dorado turned and disappeared in the purple water like a glittering bullet.

Juan was laughing as Raúl pulled himself onto the raft, with streams of water running down his beard. Raúl laughed too, and was not discouraged. They then discussed different ideas about how to capture a fish, and they decided that the best way was to take some of the leftover strands from the lines and tie a four-foot length to each corner of the net. That way each man could hold one strand in either hand and, with their backs to each other, they would lower the net until it hung in the water, several feet under the raft, weighed down with Juan's belt buckle, which they tied at the center. This idea seemed to have a number of virtues; one of the chief ones was that it allowed them to sit in a comfortable position while they waited for the fish.

As the clumps of sargasso floated by, they picked them up and shook out the little crustaceans over the holes at the center of the inner tubes. Then they began to put some of the seaweed there to make it more realistic and enticing for the fish. After a while, schools of pinfish gathered under the raft and began feeding. Raúl encouraged them by picking out little crabs, cracking the shells between his teeth, and spitting them into the water.

Above them, a frigate bird looked down on the raft as it glided in wide circles, barely flapping its long, elegant black wings. Juan and Raúl did not notice the bird. They squinted as they looked into the water with great concentration. The sun was lower now, and its light more subdued. A warm breeze blew from the south and it felt soft and pleasant.

Under a drifting island of sargasso, Raúl saw another dorado. It was a female and not as big as the first one. Still, it looked over two feet long, and Raúl could see its flank glistening in the slanted light of the afternoon. He tensed as the yellow island floated near the raft.

"Don't move, Juan. There's one under those weeds. Maybe she'll pay us a visit."

They slowly lowered the net even farther, to make sure there was plenty of room between the net and the bottom of the raft for the fish to swim in, should it decide to come over and inspect. The dorado appeared to be in no hurry to go anywhere, and for a moment it looked as if it was going to stay in the shade of the passing sargasso. But as the floating island drifted away, the dorado suddenly turned and darted under the inner tubes. With the fish suspended under them between the hanging net and the bottom of the raft, they argued in whispers whether it would be better to raise the net in one quick motion or to bring it up gradually until the penultimate moment. They decided that even their quickest action would be no match for the explosive speed of the dorado.

Then, with great patience, Juan and Raúl began to raise the net gradually, almost imperceptibly, while they kept an eye on the fish through the gaps between the clumps of sargasso that they had placed in the holes at the center of the inner tubes. The fish nibbled on the miniature animals in the sargasso unaware of—or unconcerned about—the approaching net.

"Do you think she can see that the net is coming closer?" Raúl whispered.

"Don't know."

"She seems so damned calm and unruffled—almost cocky, like she's taunting us."

"Wouldn't you be, if you had her speed?"

As the net was about to brush against the dorado's tail, Raúl yelled, "Now!" and they quickly yanked up the four corners of the net, pressing it tightly against the bottom of Raúl's inner tube. At the same time, still holding on to the lines, Raúl threw himself across the inner tube, covering the hole in the middle with his huge chest. All hell broke loose as the fish desperately tried to escape. The dorado leaped out of the water and bounced off Raúl's chest. It then shot straight down and pushed against the net. Coming back up, it swam in frantic circles around the inside rim of the inner tube, beating the water into a froth with its tail as small clumps of sargasso flew all over the place.

"Grab her, Juan! Grab her!" Raúl yelled.

"How? I can't let go of the lines!"

"See if you can hold two in one hand! But, whatever you do, don't let the net go slack!"

Juan held both of his lines tightly against the inner tube with his left hand, and reached in for the fish with his right. Again and again he grabbed at the fish, but each time the fish slipped between his fingers.

"Grab the gills! See if you can grab her by the gills!" Raúl yelled.

The dorado leaped again, and as it hit Raúl's chest, Juan managed to get his hand around the bottom of the fish and slip his fingers under the gill covers. He squeezed with all his strength and felt the delicate structures inside the gills break and the blood begin to run on his hand and drip down into the water. The fish, feeling the pain, shook violently and Juan pinned it against Raúl's chest and held it there. He could hear the tail slapping against Raúl's body, and in his hand he felt the spasms of the fish in its death struggle. After a while the convulsive shaking stopped, and then Juan felt a gentle tremor as life left the dorado.

"We got her, Raúl! Your net worked!" said Juan. "And what a fish! Look at those colors!"

Juan handed the fish to Raúl, his hands trembling. He then pulled the net from the water and folded it across his lap, and they laid the dorado on it. Even as they were admiring it, the colors began to fade and in moments turned into an ugly gray, almost as dark as charcoal at the top, and lighter, but just as dull and lifeless, along the sides.

Raúl took the knife from his pocket and slit the fish's belly, and a handful of fish eggs spilled on Juan's lap. As Juan held the fish, Raúl scooped up the clumps of roe, letting only a few shiny yellow eggs dribble into the water. Raúl ate the roe slowly, savoring each salty lump, first rolling and then squashing the tiny eggs between his tongue and the roof of his mouth. Reaching into the cavity with two fingers, Raúl cleaned out the remaining eggs and shared them with Juan. He then made the slit bigger, thrust his whole hand into the belly of the fish, and began to pull out the organs. They ate the liver and all the other soft parts and found most of them good and sweet except for a few bitter pieces, which they spit into the water.

Then Raúl carved a fillet of white meat from one side, starting at the top next to the dorsal fin, and cutting down along the ribs. He cut the meat in little chunks and they ate their fill, finishing all the meat from one side. Feeling strong and full of life now, with the essence of the fish coursing through his veins, Raúl cut out the meat from the other side in one big slab more than a foot long and almost an inch thick at the top. He dipped it in the water to clean off the blood and, without scaling it, he secured it to the inner tube using two strands from the rope.

When he finished with the fish, he watched the disk of the sun descend toward the western horizon. And as the last shining remnant of the uppermost rim vanished into the sea, Raúl saw the quick flash of green light that sometimes comes at sunset on very clear evenings when the air has been cleaned and purified by the passage of a great storm.

Chapter

Eight

A heavy jolt awoke Juan. At first he thought they had struck rocks, and he sprang up and sat stiffly, peering into the dark water. But he saw no rocks. The surface of the water was smooth and unbroken. Everything was still, and the only thing he heard was the muffled sound the inner tubes made against the water as they moved slightly when he shifted his position to look over his shoulder.

He shook Raúl, who was already awake.

"Did you feel that, Raúl?"

"Yes, what was it?"

"Don't know, felt like we hit a rock."

"See anything?"

"No."

The blow came again, and this time it was followed by a wet squeaking sound as the back of a shark rubbed against the underside of the raft. The skin of the shark was solid and rough, and it felt as though the inner tubes were being dragged over barely submerged rocks or concrete pilings. In the darkness, the shark did not feel like a living thing.

An arm's length away from the raft, Juan saw a swirling phosphorescence as the shark passed under them. The glowing whirlpool lingered on the surface of the water while the full length of the shark slipped beneath the raft. Then he saw the edge of a fin moving away, cleaving the still water. His eyes followed the thin line and saw it turn broadside twenty feet from them. The outline of the fin showed ghostly white in the starlight as it began to cut a circle around them on the surface of the water.

The shark circled twice, and then the dorsal fin dipped lower and disappeared. It was a tiger shark with a very broad, squared-off head. At either end of its shovel-shaped snout it had large, wide-open nostrils that looked more like the nostrils of a horse than the usual small nostrils that most sharks have, and they were covered by ugly flaps of skin that fluttered as the shark moved through the water. It was sixteen feet long and must have weighed over a thousand pounds. Its jaws were a foot wider than a man's shoulders and were filled with rows of serrated teeth that were notched on one side and angled on the other, like the comb of a rooster. It had a ravenous appetite and was one of the few sharks that, like the great white, sometimes attacked boats and other things floating on the water.

Juan could not see it now as it moved toward the raft, several feet under the surface. But soon he felt another bump. This one was more tentative, almost gentle, then the shark turned away and slid deeper into the water.

"Is he gone?" Raúl asked.

"There!" Juan yelled. "See? There's the fin! No, over *there!*" he said, pointing toward a dark shape moving on the surface.

Then they heard a rippling sound as the shark gained speed and the dorsal fin raised spray, splitting the water. Juan followed the dim white spray circling the raft.

"You think he can smell the fish?" Raúl asked.

"What?"

"The fish, the fish I tied to the inner tube."

"No, well . . ."

As he said that, Juan yanked the slab of dorado from under the ropes lashed around Raúl's inner tube, and flung it at the shark. It splashed a few feet in front of its snout, but the shark, paying no attention to the piece of fish meat, kept circling.

Again and again it circled them and then, suddenly, Juan saw it turn and head straight toward them before it disappeared once more into the dark water.

"He's coming at us, Raúl! He's coming straight at us! Look!" Juan yelled as he watched a green phosphorescent streak rushing toward them about eight feet under the surface.

The shark came under the raft at speed and, without slowing, arched its body and shot straight up. The flat snout crashed against the bottom of Raúl's inner tube, flipping the raft and tossing them through the air. It then turned on its back, showing its pale belly just under the surface, and bit into Raúl's inner tube, tearing it to pieces.

Treading water a few feet away, Juan could see the one good inner tube, still inflated and lashed to what remained of Raúl's, dragging back and forth across the surface enveloped in a cloud of spray as the shark jerked its head from side to side in violent spasms, all the while clicking its huge jaws and tearing chunks of rubber from the deflated inner tube.

"Let go, you bastard! Let go!" Raúl yelled.

As he shouted, Raúl began to swim toward the inner tube that was still throwing up walls of spray each time the shark jerked it across the water.

"Stop, Raúl! Stop! He'll kill you!" Juan called.

"If he tears the other one up, it'll be over anyway!" Raúl yelled back.

In his rage, Raúl swam toward the shark. When he was halfway between Juan and the shark, the inner tube stopped moving. The surface of the water became still again, and everything turned quiet. Raúl stopped in midstroke, letting his legs drop under him, and his motionless body hung suspended for a moment in the water. He then began to adjust his position, moving his legs like scissors, as he scanned the surface of the water around him looking for a sign of the shark.

The sea was like a sheet of glass. Thirty feet away from him he could see the silhouette of the inner tube against a patch of stars hanging low over the eastern horizon.

A few minutes passed, and then Juan whispered, "Do you see him?"

"No."

"Can you reach the inner tube?"

Raúl did not answer as his eyes skimmed the surface of

the water. The inner tube was now drifting away from him, and Raúl began once again to swim toward it in a smooth breaststroke. With his head high above the water, he kept looking all around him while he swam.

A light breeze ruffled the water now and blew the inner tube farther away. Raúl picked up his pace as the breeze teased him, pushing the inner tube out of his reach whenever he came close.

Then the breeze blew stronger and Raúl broke into a crawl, chasing after the tube. His big arms came down hard, beating the water with each stroke, and his legs churned the water, leaving a frothy trail behind him.

Raúl was now within reach of the inner tube, and he gave a few powerful strokes and lunged toward it. As his right hand grasped a line, the water under the inner tube exploded and the head of the shark burst out in front of him. Raúl let out a scream as the snout struck his chest and pushed him back, whirling through the water, out of the way of the massive animal. The shark's momentum carried it past him, and for a moment Raúl could see the back of the shark just under the water, speeding away from him into the darkness. Then he saw the dorsal fin, as wide as a door at the base, turn around and head toward him, slicing the surface and throwing up spray.

Raúl saw the water bulge before him, and as the shark came upon him, he stretched his arms out, trying to fend off the attack, and jammed a finger deep into the fleshy nostril on the left side. The shark turned its head away from the offending finger, and Raúl saw its black eye turn white as the nictitating membrane closed over it. Then the shark circled back and flipped on its side as it came toward him.

And Raúl saw the blurry outline of the jaws as they opened beneath him, showing the enormous, all-devouring black cavity against the pale underbelly.

Juan had followed Raúl, swimming behind him. And now, as he moved closer, he felt something that does not carry a name. Something that had lingered like a vapor in the secret memories of his childhood. Juan could not explain it and he did not understand it because there was nothing to understand, nothing to explain. He had been afraid and now he was not. And how do you explain such a crossing? From darkness to light, from death to life. How do you explain such a thing?

Raúl turned toward Juan and shouted, "*¡Atrás!* Go back!"

But Juan swam closer, closer, until he sensed the swirl and bulge of the water ahead of the onrushing shark. As the shark came at Raúl, Juan grasped a pectoral fin and struck the gills hard with his fist before reeling back from the force of the moving shark.

Then he saw the strange, broad teeth thrust out and the jaws close around Raúl's waist, ripping the flesh and sinking deep into his abdominal muscles. And he saw Raúl lifted clear above the surface and shoved down headfirst into the water, only to be raised again as the shark shook its head back and forth, back and forth.

In the starlight Juan saw the rippling lateral muscles of the shark as its whole body convulsed and he saw Raúl struggling, striking the shark, his dark blood staining the white underbelly every time the shark raised its head out of the water. Then Juan heard the crunching sound of bones snapping as Raúl's ribs and spinal column cracked, and the noise the bones made when they snapped was louder than Juan ever imagined such a sound would be. And he saw the jaws open very wide and then shut tight, severing Raúl's body in half.

The bloody severed torso fell from the mouth of the shark and floated on the surface for a moment before the shark opened its mouth again and swallowed what remained of Raúl in a single bite.

Then the shark dove back into the depths and the ripples on the water faded until the surface was flat again and there was only silence and the light of the stars reflected on the sea.

Numb with shock, Juan swam to the remaining inner tube that was floating nearby, grabbed a line, and towed it back to the spot where he thought Raúl had last been. But there was no way of really knowing that the place he swam back to was the exact spot, and even in his confused state, he was aware that he could not know.

Still, he imagined that he was back at the place in the sea where Raúl had been, because he felt a great need to be there—as if all the fear and all the death and all the duplicity of the last thirty years had been swallowed in that place, had vanished in that place.

Then he thought that even if he had come back to the same place where Raúl had been, the current was carrying him away from there, and it made him anxious and for a moment he started swimming against the current. But then he thought that the current carried everything with it, just as it had carried him and the raft together as he swam toward it, keeping their relative positions the same as it swept them along, and the only thing that made a difference was the wind. But there was no wind now, so everything must be moving together, even the exact spot, which had to be moving with him now, right with him, and below him, and all around him.

The thought that both he and the place where Raúl had been were flowing together in the Gulf Stream brought him a mysterious comfort—filled him with a confidence that he was sure came from Raúl. And even as he felt the comfort and the confidence, he knew that it made no sense.

Then he thought that he might be going crazy, but he realized in a flash that he was aware of the strangeness of the ideas that filled his mind, and this meant that he was not mad. And that very realization almost brought him back to his old world, but he saw the door begin to open and he caught a glimpse of the horror behind it and he knew that he did not want to face it. So he shut the door and thought that the water felt warmer over the place, and he even reached out and touched the other water outside the place and felt that it was, indeed, colder, which meant that he was still where he was supposed to be.

Chapter Nine

The alarm clock rang and Carmen stretched, turned it off, and lay on her back a few minutes before walking across her bedroom to the bathroom. The tile floor felt cold against her bare feet. Before stepping into the shower, she slipped off her short blue silk nightgown and stood naked before the full-length mirror while she let the hot water run, warming the tub. She waited until the steam began to fog the mirror, blurring the reflection of her body, and then stepped under the shower. The warm water felt good as it ran through her hair and down the curve of her back, softly caressing her glistening buttocks.

As she lathered, Carmen moved with the natural, almost haughty confidence that beautiful women everywhere always move with. At thirty, her body was nearing the ripe perfection it would reach in the next decade, but it already exuded a sweetness that unseasoned younger women lack.

She toweled herself dry and dressed while she watched a Spanish-language television newscast. The strong aroma of espresso coffee filled the small apartment, and the first rays of the sun filtered through the vertical blinds, casting parallel shadows on the white tile floor of the living room. The apartment was immaculately clean and perfectly ordered. The furniture was sparse but elegant. Everything seemed light and cheerful, and there was an open feeling about the place that made it seem much larger than it actually was.

Carmen picked up the portrait of Vivian's son and examined it once more in the sunlight. She had worked and reworked the eyes, and now she was finally satisfied with them. They were strong, confident eyes that, when the time came, would return to rebuild a homeland they had never seen.

In the exhilarating atmosphere of Miami, Carmen had sat through many heated discussions about the anticipated post-Castro transition to democracy, and had heard countless experts debate the process of privatization. But she knew that those light brown eyes looking back at her now, and hundreds of thousands like them, would do more to restore *La Patria*—"the Fatherland"—than the millions of dollars in goods and services tugging at the bit now, ready to rush south across the Straits to begin the reconstruction.

From the moment she arrived in Miami, Carmen had been filled with pride at the obvious success of the Cuban exiles. Growing up in Cuba, a child of the revolution, she had heard so many contradictory things about American society and the Cuban exiles in Miami that she did not know what to expect, what life in Miami would truly be like, or how she, a well-known artist who had worked for Castro's propaganda machine, would be received by the Cubans living in the United States.

In the late sixties, when she was a schoolgirl in Havana, she had been taught that the Cuban expatriates had it very bad in Miami. Castro always referred to the Cubans who left after the revolution as *gusanos,* which means "worms." At first he told the Cubans on the island that the *gusanos* in the United States were treated badly, that they were shunned by the Americans, that they were poor and lived in ghettos and led miserable, lonely lives. A well-deserved fate in the eyes of Castro. And if things were bad in Cuba, the Cubans on the island at least had the comfort that it was worse for the Cuban exiles in Miami, or so they were told. After all, in Cuba, under Fidel's leadership, they were building socialism. Hardships in Cuba had to be expected, they were natural, they came with the territory. But back then they had something to look forward to, they had a future. A glorious revolutionary future, and they were sure to achieve it, against all odds. That was what she was taught as a child. And she believed it then. She firmly believed they would succeed.

Had Fidel not defeated the Yankees at the Bay of Pigs during the battle of Playa Girón? That was undeniable. She had seen the films of the American warships off the coast, and of the enemy airplanes blown to pieces by Castro's air force. And she had heard tapes of the intercepted radio communications by the desperate men on the beach, surrounded, outgunned, calling for air support amid the massacre, begging the Yankees for air cover that never came.

And she had seen the American warships turn and run, out of harm's way, abandoning the bloodied men, leaving behind the body-littered beach of Playa Girón. Yes, Fidel had defeated the Yankees, that was obvious.

Then, later, when she was a student at the university, she had actually met Cuban exiles from Miami when the exiles began visiting Cuba for the first time since the revolution, during a brief period of warmer relations between Cuba and the United States in the mid-seventies.

Meeting these free Cubans was a great shock to her, and it changed her life forever. Contrary to what she had been told all these years, the exiles did not appear poor or miserable. They were well dressed, they looked happy, and they brought so many things with them, so many wonderful things. And they gave everything away to their relatives and friends and sometimes to strangers on the streets. The exiles gave away clothes, medicines, makeup, electronic gadgets. Some of them even gave away their suitcases and returned to Miami with only the clothes they wore.

Carmen never forgot the day her schoolmate, Susana, came over, all excited, to model some underwear that a distant cousin visiting from Miami had given her. Susana tried on several pairs of panties, each time strutting around the room, naked except for the panties, and swinging her hips in an exaggerated way. Each pair was a different color, and they were all cut high around the legs and accentuated Susana's youthful feminine thighs and tight rear. Then Susana put on a black underwire bra that was a little big for her, and asked Carmen to try it on.

It was a perfect fit, and, looking into the mirror at her full round breasts, gently held up by the cups, with the dark erect nipples showing clearly through the lace, Carmen felt like a woman for the first time in her life. Seeing how perfectly the bra fit, Susana, suddenly overcome with generosity, gave it to her, and for years it was one of Carmen's most prized possessions. She wore it only on special occasions and always wrapped it carefully afterwards and hid it in a special place, a secret cubbyhole that she cut out behind her bookcase only for that purpose. After a while the bra became a symbol to her, and she always thought about it when she thought about the contradictions in the speeches of Fidel.

Then she began to wear it under her dull outer clothing every time she was forced to attend a mass rally and listen to Castro drone on about building socialism. And she thought that wearing it during those rallies almost qualified as a private protest, and she often fantasized about climbing onto the podium, stripping off her blouse, and showing off the American bra to the astonished crowd. That fantasy, and other equally outrageous ones, kept her mind occupied and amused through the stifling heat and boredom of the rallies.

The telephone rang as Carmen was going out the door, and she rushed back to answer it. It was Andrés's daughter, Margarita.

"They've left."

Carmen hesitated for a moment. She felt lightheaded, and the tips of her fingers began to tingle.

"Are you sure?"

"I just talked with Rogelio. He's in Cojímar. He told me that when he last saw them, about a week ago, they were headed east, toward Guanabo."

"When did they leave?"

"He doesn't know. But he has not seen any of them since then. He said Juan has not been at the university since Monday. The G-2 is looking for him and for my father and for a third man who left with them, Raúl. Rogelio didn't know his last name," said Margarita.

"I was going to have breakfast with Vivian at Versailles on Eighth Street—do you know her? She's an officer with the Coast Guard."

"Yes, yes. She's always been so kind."

"Can you meet us there?"

"Of course. I'm on my way."

Every morning, as she drove down Brickell Avenue, Carmen enjoyed looking at the buildings lining Biscayne Bay. She specially liked the bolder, more colorful ones resplendent in the early sunlight reflected off the bay. Up close, from the road, the colors were so powerful that they seemed outrageous—a cacophony of shades. But from afar, out on the water or looking down from an airplane, the buildings came alive. From that distance the great buildings moved and changed with the light and seemed to dance.

Today Carmen did not see the buildings. She did not see anything else as she drove down Brickell Avenue, weaving desperately through the morning traffic. She did not think—she refused to think—about Juan and the others adrift on the Gulf Stream. She only wanted to get to Vivian and . . . and what? She did not know what.

The scent of freshly baked Cuban bread mixed with the steamy aroma of *café con leche* and floated over the crowded restaurant. Dark-haired men in silk suits or heavily starched traditional *guayaberas* sat around small tables engaged in heated conversations, driving home each point with expansive gestures.

Carmen spotted Vivian and Margarita at a table near the kitchen and made her way toward them, carrying the portrait of Vivian's son. There was a hush at each table as Carmen walked by and the men stopped in mid-sentence and centered their attention first on her body and then on her eyes, which, in the low light toward the back of the restaurant, were deep violet and full of pain. And after they saw her eyes the men looked away and did not smile or make any comments as they normally would, but remained silent.

Vivian spoke first.

"Margarita told me they left."

"Are you *sure?*" Carmen asked, sounding more accusatory than she meant to, and fixing her eyes on Margarita's with such intensity that Margarita looked down and played with her teaspoon for a moment before answering.

"Rogelio said they left from Guanabo," said Margarita.

"Did he *see* them go?" asked Carmen.

"No, but Juan told him they were going to try to leave through Guanabo that night or the next, and asked Rogelio to call one of us. Juan told Rogelio that he had tried to call you, but could not get a call out. It's getting almost impossible to get a call out—you know how it is."

"What day did Rogelio see them?"

"Last Sunday . . . five days ago."

"The day before the . . ."

Carmen did not finish the sentence. She felt clammy and cold and began to shudder as the hopelessness of the situation broke over her like a dam bursting and overwhelmed her with such force that she could not speak. But then out of her despair a familiar feeling began to rise like a fine wind blowing from a secret place.

"Vivian, do you think there is any way?"

"I know of at least one confirmed case," said Vivian. "A few years ago, four men on an inner-tube raft were picked up by a freighter in the Old Bahama Channel. They had been carried nearly two hundred miles to the east by a hurricane."

"They survived the hurricane?" Margarita asked, her voice rising.

"There have been other stories, but this one was definitely confirmed by the freighter captain." Vivian kept her tone level and maintained the same cool, professional detachment she used while briefing her staff. "He had tracked the hurricane, and based on where the men had left and where he picked them up, there was no question that they were carried by the hurricane."

"I think I remember reading something about it," said Margarita.

"Yes, it was all over the papers, and one of the networks even wanted to do a special on them. But the men had relatives in Cuba and they were afraid their families would be harassed, so they refused to be interviewed."

"And there have been other stories of survivors? You know of other cases—on rafts?" Carmen asked with growing enthusiasm.

"Yes, I'm familiar with other cases of people who have escaped on rafts and survived hurricanes, many other cases," said Vivian.

She lied about the "many," and she did not talk about the empty rafts she had seen over the years as a Coast Guard officer, but she thought about them. And she remembered the first time she had spotted one of those sad, flimsy things adrift on the Gulf Stream.

Vivian had been a young petty officer then, at the helm of a cutter, and when she first saw it she thought it was only another piece of garbage carried by the current, just more refuse from some unknown shore. So her first reaction to the thing was one of irritation, and she began to mumble something about how bad the pollution was getting on the high seas. But as she steered clear of it, she recognized what it was, and all at once, without expecting it, without preparation, she came face to face with all the stories that Cuban children in Miami grow up reading, mostly in Spanish—fantastic stories of men and women, and sometimes children, wading into the sea late at night grasping an inner tube or a piece of wood or a chunk of Styrofoam, dousing themselves with kerosene to fend off sharks, and floating into the darkness.

Once she had even heard a crazy story about a man who set out from Baracoa into the Gulf Stream on his horse. He had spent days carving four big flippers out of yagua—which is what Cubans call the bud shields of the royal palm. When his neighbors asked him what he was making, he told them that they were horse flippers, which he was going to strap to the legs of his horse and ride to Miami. His neighbors shook their heads and laughed and poked fun at the man. Then one evening, after the sun had set, when the sky was still light and the sea was purple, they saw the man riding his horse into the water and ran up a small hill by the shore and yelled out to him. But the man did not answer them, and they never saw him again.

But even after all the stories she had read and heard, Vivian was not ready to see what she saw that first time because, attached to one of the inner tubes, by a rope around his wrists, was the body of a man. And when they pulled him out, they realized that it was only the upper torso, because something had eaten the bottom half.

And now Vivian thought about that first time and felt the horror all over again, but she hid her feelings well, just as she had done so many years ago when she was the only woman and the only Cuban in the cutter.

"Vivian, is there anything . . ." Carmen was not sure what she was going to ask, or what Vivian could do.

"I've already notified stations from Key West to Port Canaveral," said Vivian. "I called as soon as Margarita told me. I also asked my staff to tell all the marinas to put the word out to the charter boat captains."

"I hate to ask, Vivian, you have done so much already, but is there anything else . . ." said Carmen.

"I can't think . . . well, yes, there is. I can call Alberto."

"Who's Alberto?"

"He owns a flight school in Marathon. He escaped in a small airplane back in the sixties, and he's always on the lookout for raft people."

Chapter *Ten*

Juan was floating facedown with his head halfway in the shade at the center of the inner tube. It was a very small shade and would soon disappear as the sun rose higher, but it was the only shade for miles, and it protected his eyes for now from the morning glare. His body was swollen. There were painful welts on his legs from jellyfish stings, and his face was puffed up like a blowfish with open sores that oozed bloody pus.

The sun was very hot even at this time in the morning, and there was hardly any wind, which made it even hotter. The black surface of the inner tube was covered with white spots of caked salt crystals where the sun had dried the seawater. He tried to remain still, because each time he shifted position he burned his bare, sun-blistered arms against the rubber.

Looking down into the clear water, he could see what remained of the net Raúl had made, moving limply under the inner tube. His belt buckle was still attached to the bottom of the net, and in the slanted shafts of the morning light it shone greenish gold. Around the net flashed a bright-colored cloud of tropical fish, feeding on the tiny shrimp and crabs that crawled along the mesh. The cloud expanded and contracted and changed colors as it swirled like a watery kaleidoscope.

Fifty thousand feet above him, a military jet streaked silently, painting a thin white contrail against the sky. From that altitude the pilot could see the deep purplish color of the Gulf Stream and the thin, serpentine line separating its currents from the shallow littoral waters, which showed a light green. North of the line the pilot could see the Florida Keys, a string of small, irregular green islands arcing gently to the northeast, toward the mainland. Right about the middle of the string of islands, Marathon airstrip showed clearly like a thin white chalk line set off against the greenness of Vaca Key.

On the ramp south of the airstrip, Alberto was standing next to a little single-engine Cessna, going over the preflight check procedure as a young female student pilot listened attentively and followed him around the airplane.

"Look here. See the cotter pin securing this nut to the flap hinge?" he asked as they both crouched under the wing.

"Yes."

"Always look for cotter pins—nice and tight. No cotter pins, no fly. Okay?"

"Okay."

Alberto was around the other side, reaching into the open cowling to drain fuel from the sediment bulb, when the telephone rang inside his office, and he went to answer it.

"Alberto? Vivian. We have a reliable report of three who put to sea five days ago at Guanabo."

"Boat?"

"No. Inner-tube raft."

"¡Dios mio!" he gasped. "There's no way, with the hurricane."

"I know the family."

"Five days ago?"

"Yes."

"Where?"

"Guanabo Beach—just east of Havana."

"Okay. I was just about to take off with a student. I'll tell the other pilots."

The ground fell away and Alberto saw the number 25, upside down, three hundred feet below him on the concrete, as the little aircraft cleared the far end of the runway and headed skyward, guided by the student pilot seated to his left. The airplane jerked left and right and up and down as the fledgling pilot overcorrected for every bump and air pocket caused by the rising columns of air over the hot concrete.

"Relax. Don't hold the yoke so tight," said Alberto. "Remember what I told you, the airplane wants to fly. She's not going to fall from the sky. She *wants* to fly. Just like a horse wants to gallop. Do you know how to ride a horse?"

"Yes."

"The airplane is just like a horse. You have to be firm but

gentle. Don't jerk the controls. Be smooth, real smooth. Just let her know where you want to go, and let her handle the terrain. Like you do a horse. Okay?"

"Okay."

"You're doing fine—real good!" he added with a grandfatherly grin.

"Thanks."

"Turn right now, to the south, heading one-eight-zero."

The Cessna crossed the shoreline, and Alberto asked his student to level off lower than they normally did. This time, as they flew over the fishing boats, they could see the people moving around the open cockpits where the fighting chairs were. From that altitude it was more interesting and more personal, and they could sense the excitement and anticipation of the fishermen as they sped toward deeper waters, throttles wide open, to a place where each hoped to find billfish.

Leaving the bright green coastal waters behind, the little airplane came across the edge of the Stream, and Alberto remembered the day he left Cuba. He was thirty then, and working as a spray-plane pilot for a government farm. The farm's previous owners had escaped after the National Institute for Agrarian Reform confiscated their farm, and they'd left behind several airplanes.

One was a brand-new Twin Cessna 310 that had caught the eye of the *comandante* in charge of agrarian reform, and he had ordered it flown immediately to Havana to be used as his personal airplane. There was no time to fly in a military pilot to pick it up. The *comandante* wanted it *now.* He had a date that night and he wanted to impress her with this new toy he had stolen from the *latifundistas,* as the

Communists called the large landholders. Alberto was the logical choice to fly it; he was the only pilot on the farm who had a multi-engine rating, and he seemed reliable. They were less careful back then.

Alberto topped off the tanks and climbed into the cockpit, which still smelled new. He left the grass strip near Ciego de Avila, in the center of the island about two hundred forty miles east of Havana, and headed for the capital. They did not have Soviet radar back then, and they were not very well organized, but they followed him on the radio and asked him to report his position and altitude on a regular basis.

When he was halfway to Havana, he called Havana control and reported, "Twin Cessna CUN-two-two-three, ten thousand feet over Sagua la Grande." The controller responded, "Two-two-three, report over Cardenas."

Alberto then put the microphone back on its holder next to the trim control and turned toward the north coast, which was twelve miles off his right wingtip. As he flew over the mangrove-covered cays and islets hugging the coast, he pushed the nose down and dove toward the water without throttling back. The sky disappeared from his windshield, replaced by the deeper blue of the Gulf Stream, and he watched the airspeed indicator needle swing out of the green arc into the yellow arc and approach the red "never exceed" line as the aircraft accelerated smoothly, trading altitude for airspeed, in its dive toward the surface of the sea. He waited until the very last moment before he pulled back on the yoke and leveled the Cessna a few feet above the crests of the waves, feeling the G's as his body pushed against the bottom of the seat.

Forty-five minutes later the radio crackled, "Twin Cessna CUN-two-two-three, Havana Control, report Cardenas. You should be over Cardenas."

Alberto reached for the microphone and then stopped. But when he heard the controller again, saying, "Cessna CUN-two-two-three, report Cardenas," he could not resist.

"Havana, Cessna CUN-two-two-three, cannot report Cardenas."

"Two-two-three, report position. Are you lost?"

"Negative, I have the field in sight."

"What field?"

"Marathon field."

"Cessna CUN-two-two-three, say again, what field?"

"Marathon airfield, Florida Keys, *Estados Unidos de Norte America.*"

"Cessna CUN-two-two- . . ."

Alberto switched frequencies and, in the best English he could muster, spoke into the microphone, "Miami Center, Twin Cessna Charlie Uniform November two-two-three, fifteen miles south of Marathon, advise immigration requesting asylum, request landing instructions . . ."

That was almost thirty years ago, but he remembered every detail. He remembered the way the sunlight reflected off the metal hook on the back of the microphone when he picked it up, and the pleasant new smell inside the cockpit, and how comfortable and quick his flight had been. And he smiled as he always smiled when he thought about that flight across the straits almost thirty years ago. But he also felt guilty because it had been so easy for him.

For him the flight had been not so much an escape as a great adventure, a going forth, he thought. He always told ultimate price. Others thought the word had been "Cuba," the beloved *Patria* the boy had left behind.

But the journalist personally thought the word had been "mother." He thought that, in his last moment, the boy had tried to call his mother, as all children do when they are hurt. And, of course, no one knew who his mother was or whether she had left with him on the raft and had died along the way or had stayed behind and was now sobbing quietly, terrified and alone, in some desolate corner of the island. And the eyes of the people filled with tears when he said that, and the speaker himself choked up and for a few moments the only thing that could be heard was the sound of all the flags fluttering in the wind.

Chapter *Eleven*

Before falling asleep, Juan had wrapped a line around his wrists to keep from slipping off the inner tube, and now he was dreaming of the wind. In his dream he saw the ripples on the water as the wind stroked the water the way a man caresses a woman. Then he felt himself lifted above the water and carried by the wind, and his dream was so vivid that he felt in his stomach as though he were truly flying and he saw the white crests of the waves pass under him at great speed. But the burning pain from the jellyfish stings awoke him before he finished his dream.

The pain annoyed him now not so much for its unpleasantness but because it did not let him sleep, and lately when he was awake he only thought about death, which he considered to have already begun and now it was only a matter of seeing it through to its conclusion. He was not sad about death and he was not frightened. Nor did the loneliness bother him. Besides, he thought that he was not truly lonely as long as someone cared for him and he knew that even now Carmen was caring for him and perhaps other people he did not know were caring for him. He also still felt connected to Raúl in a strange way, and he felt that what he thought and what he did continued to affect Raúl, the same way Raúl was affecting him now as he flowed in the current. So he did not feel lonely and he did not feel sad because he considered himself already a dead man. But he continued to think about death and wondered if dying was different from what anyone supposed, if perhaps it was a good thing, a lucky thing. He wondered if Andrés knew that death was lucky, perhaps luckier than life, and had reconciled himself to it when he said, "It's the only way." He thought he had. His voice had sounded strange, as if it came from another world. But maybe that was just the nature of his voice, he thought. Andrés had been a preacher of sorts, and they have voices like that.

Whether Andrés had or not, Juan could not reconcile himself to death, and since that was all he thought about now when he was awake, being awake bothered him. So he forced himself to concentrate on the swirling patterns of many-colored fish swimming around the net until he could no longer see the individual fish, but only the changing colors. The colors mesmerized him, and after a while he was asleep again and dreaming of the wind.

In his dream he was aloft once more and felt the familiar butterflies in his stomach, but this time he was over fields of sugarcane and he saw the fingers of the wind stroking the tall stalks of cane. And as the wind stroked the cane, he saw how the fields changed colors from a deep green to a lighter green where the wind passed. The rippling colors reflected the ebb and flow of the wind as it moved over the great fields that extended to the horizon in all directions.

Juan knew that this was a childhood dream in the strange way that you know certain things in dreams because now, looking down on the fields, he felt as he had when he was very young and climbed a framboyán tree every day to sit on a high branch that was broad and smooth where he waited in the coolness of the midday shade for the wind that always came in the afternoon.

He started climbing the framboyán tree after they took his father away, and at first he scanned the horizon for weeks looking for his father's return. Then his mother told him that his father would never return because the uniformed men who took him away had killed him. But he continued to climb the tree even after she told him, and he continued to scan the horizon every day until after sunset when it became too dark to keep looking, and after a while he learned the habits of the wind.

For the rest of that year he continued to climb the framboyán tree. But by then he had stopped looking for his father and climbed only to wait for the coming of the wind, which always came without warning early in the afternoon.

And now in his dream he felt the wind blowing again through his secret place, caressing his face, stirring his hair and rustling the great stalks of cane until they became as fluid and impermanent as the waves in the ocean. And he remembered, as you remember things in dreams, that the only thing that was constant and reliable in those days was the wind that came in the afternoon and then moved away until it disappeared over the horizon, leaving the fields still and flat again, like a green, tranquil sea.

When the wind stopped, Juan knew he had finished his dream and he felt the same longing that he felt when he was a boy and thought that the wind was connected in some mysterious way with his father and that every day after sunset the wind went searching for the place where his father was now and reached that place at an appointed time.

Chapter Twelve

The sun had risen farther, and now it shone almost straight down on the water. Alberto had dropped off his student at the airstrip, refueled, and taken the Cessna back out. This time he was by himself. He could not concentrate on the search with the student next to him. Besides, it was unfair to her, although she had been enthusiastic enough and willing to help when he told her.

He headed southwest, toward Key West, flying over the edge of the Stream. Earlier he had covered the area around the middle Keys, searching inside a long rectangle that went from Boot Key south to Sombrero Key light, then northeast along the edge of the stream all the way to the light at Tennessee Reef, then toward the shore to Long Key and back down to Boot Key. After that he had searched a similar-sized rectangle but farther off shore, from Sombrero Key light south to about fifteen miles over the Gulf Stream, then northeast until he was about even with Tennessee Reef, back in toward Tennessee Reef, then south again to Sombrero Key.

He scanned the surface with great intensity, attentive to the slightest break in the blue monotony, the merest hint of something—anything—floating on the water. Sometimes his eyes would catch a glimmer, a flash, a change in the way the sunlight reflected off the water, and Alberto would pull back on the throttle, slip down closer to the surface, and slowly circle the spot. A piece of plywood. The top of a Styrofoam cooler. A loose lobster-trap buoy. A yellow island of sargasso weed. A nondescript accumulation of garbage. But mostly nothing. A false reflection off a rogue wave from some passing tanker. Or his imagination, a feeling, a sudden urge that something is there. Like a fisherman who sees the silhouette of a sailfish's bill break the surface near his bait and right away tells himself he imagined it. There was nothing. I saw nothing, he says to himself just before the line flies off the outrigger.

A man is so hard to see from an airplane, Alberto thought. Sometimes a thing as insignificant as a paper plate or a yellow rag lying on the grass is easier to spot than a man walking across a field. And it is even harder if the man is in the water, he thought. Then the only thing that usually shows is a tiny speck of a head bobbing on the surface.

But Alberto's eyes were still good and he was sure that in certain ways it was easier for him to spot things from the air now than when he was younger. Over the years his eyes had grown accustomed to seeing the world from an airplane. The vast expanses did not overwhelm his senses as they had when he was younger. He was more patient now and took the time to look for subtler things. He remembered how hard it had been for him to spot his instructor on the ground during his first solo flight.

Respecting the established ritual surrounding the first solo, his instructor had not told him ahead of time that he would be soloing that day. They had spent the morning doing touch-and-go's at the airport in Santa Clara, as they had for the previous two weeks. After a particularly good landing his instructor asked him to come to a full stop on the runway. As soon as the airplane stopped, Alberto heard the door open on his instructor's side and felt the warm rush of adrenaline as he thought, This is *it.* His instructor stepped out quickly, leaned his head inside the cockpit, and told him to do three touch-and-go's. "I'll be here on the grass at the head of the runway," his instructor said. "If everything doesn't feel right on final, or if you see me waving my arms, just apply power and go around." Then his instructor smiled, shut the door, and gave Alberto a big thumbs-up. Alberto took off smoothly and gained confidence as he maneuvered the little red airplane around the pattern. As he lined her up on final, everything seemed right, but he began to look around for his instructor just to be sure. He saw nothing but a long white concrete runway surrounded by a sea of green grass. The runway came closer and loomed larger and larger. Full flaps. Airspeed okay. Still no instructor. Where is he? Is he playing a practical joke? Did he go to the bathroom? Hand on the throttle, ready to go around. Drifting to the left. Correct for the crosswind. Crab her just a little. Okay lined up again. Looks good. Where *is* he? Nothing but grass and concrete. If I don't see him I'll put her down and taxi off the runway. I won't do a touch-and-go. Okay. Almost there. Concentrate. Here we go. Begin the flare. *There! There he is!* Sitting on the grass by the runway. He's smiling. Giving me a thumbs-up! Feel the reassuring bump of the gear on the runway. Okay! Full power. Flaps up. Carburetor heat off. Here we go.

Surely a man is the hardest thing to see from the sky, Alberto thought. But he also felt great confidence. Today he felt as he had the day he left Cuba, as if there were a great, irresistible magnet out there in the blue distance, just over the horizon, drawing him toward darker waters. He had heard fishermen speak of the same thing many times. They said their prey called to them.

His plan now was to search the area around the lower Keys. He would go beyond Key West, past the Marquesas, almost to the Dry Tortugas, and then return to the middle Keys in the afternoon with the sun at his back. Now he was about seven miles out and even with Bahía Honda, where the lower Keys begin. Ahead he could see the light at Big Pine Shoal. No sense in looking around the shallows between the lights and the Keys. If they make it this far, someone is bound to see them. Earlier he had wasted time looking around the shallows off the middle Keys. But he had not wanted to take the student out too far, that would have been unfair to her.

The long row of navigational lights that begins near Miami, at Fowey Rocks, and arcs down all the way to the Tortugas, follows the curve of the Keys about six to eight miles offshore and warns passing ships of the nearby shallows and living coral reefs. Beyond the lights, the floor of the sea drops off and forms a great canyon ninety miles wide and over a mile deep. And through this canyon the Gulf Stream flows like a warm wind blowing silently through the inner spaces of the earth. The power of the Stream is so great that the huge tankers traveling westward, against the flow, hug the shallows to avoid the full force of its currents.

The sea was brighter now as the sun began to arc down toward the west, and the glare made it harder for Alberto to see. It would be better coming back with the sun behind him, he thought.

He saw more white fishing boats. Some were returning after a morning of trolling the Stream, and they passed by other boats going out. In the morning they are all going out and toward evening they are all returning, he thought, but around midday the outgoing and incoming traffic is about even. And seeing all the boats gave Alberto more confidence. If they are still alive, someone is bound to see them.

But Alberto saw nothing and flew on beyond the Sambos, beyond Sand Key, toward the Marquesas. Maybe they are around the Marquesas, where four hundred years ago a hurricane tossed the treasure-laden Spanish galleons *Nuestra Señora de Atocha* and the *Santa Margarita* against the reefs, he thought. Or maybe the storm blew them farther west, toward Rebecca around the Quicksands, or as far as the Tortugas. They must be somewhere. Unless they were blown past all that into the broad waters of the Gulf, and then nothing can save them.

When he came upon the Marquesas he went down close to the surface and flew all around and searched the water in a great circle and then searched the area around Rebecca Shoals and the Quicksands and saw nothing. Then he went as far as the Dry Tortugas, although he had not planned to because the Tortugas are farther west than Havana, and normally no one who puts to sea at Guanabo should end up at the Tortugas with the current carrying them to the northeast with all that force. But there is no telling what a hurricane can do. So Alberto searched around the Tortugas and then flew to the northwest over the still, bright waters of the Gulf for a while because the thought of these men . . . *Were* they men? Vivian had not said. She'd said she had a reliable report of three who left from Guanabo. Three what? Maybe they were women. Maybe there was a child with them. Alberto thought about the funeral in Miami and shuddered.

It is very strange to be a Cuban exile in the United States, having gone through what you have gone through and knowing what you know and seeing what you see and hearing the stories you hear every day, and still go on living a normal everyday life as if nothing were happening around you, he thought. It is like living a double life, like constantly stepping out of one universe into another and back again.

He remembered talking recently to a lady from Sancti Spiritus with a refined manner who was still very beautiful in her sixties. They were exchanging escape stories. She had been with the resistance against the Communists in 1961 and had smuggled food and weapons to the men who were fighting in the Escambray Mountains. At night she would ride a horse across the mountains, carrying saddlebags full of ammunition. During the day she taught a kindergarten class. The secret police became suspicious of her comings and goings, and when they began to close in on her, the resistance took her out in a fast boat to Islamorada in the Florida Keys to save her life. A CIA contact met her at the beach, and the men who took her out went back to Cuba. There happened to be some tourists drinking beer and having a party at the beach when the Cuban boat arrived, and the whole scene was so surreal that the tourists in their mellow stupor thought someone was filming a movie and they were too drunk to notice there were no cameras. But to the tourists it seemed like something out of a movie set. This ominous-looking launch with a .50-caliber machine gun mounted on a tripod appears out of nowhere and men in jungle gear jump into the water and help a hauntingly beautiful dark-haired woman up to the beach. At the same time a man wearing a coat and tie comes running down the beach and into the water up to his waist to meet the group. At first the tourists are frightened and don't know what to make of it. Then one of the tourists yells, "Look! It's Sophia Loren!" and everybody runs up and tries to get her autograph.

And thirty years later this lady, still hauntingly beautiful, is laughing and reminiscing with Alberto and says to him, "Can you imagine? One night I'm running arms, riding through the Escambray Mountains, scared to death, the wind blowing my hair, and the next day I'm in Islamorada with a bunch of drunk *americanos* who think I'm Sophia Loren and ask me for autographs. How can anything surprise you after that?"

But even as she laughed there was a distant sadness in her eyes and Alberto had understood her sadness because he felt it himself and he always recognized it in the eyes of others who had made the crossing and now felt a spiritual link with the ones left behind on the other shore, a sense of something unresolved, a strange wistfulness when they looked south that would not leave them even after all this time.

Alberto made a very wide circle, flying low over the Gulf, and looked in every direction and, seeing nothing, headed back south toward the Straits. It was a very clear day without even a hint of haze over the water. To his right he could see the Tortugas in the distance and the little speck that was Fort Jefferson shining in the sunlight. Closer in, around the Quicksands, a boat had run aground and was now trying to extricate itself by reversing engines. The boat churned the soft sandy bottom and the water around the boat was white, like milk of magnesia.

Looking at the gauges, Alberto saw that each tank was almost three-quarters full, but he decided to put in at Key West and top them off before heading back out over the Straits; then he would not have to come in until well after dark.

The brunt of the hurricane had missed Key West—it had passed over the water near the Tortugas—but the edge had dumped plenty of water on the city, and there was some flooding and a little damage to a few buildings under construction along the waterfront. The older buildings in the center of town were not hurt.

Most airplanes without hangar space had been flown out of harm's way before the hurricane arrived, and except for a couple of awnings that had been torn off the terminal building and some broken glass, there was not much evidence that a hurricane had come through the airport at Key West.

But water had seeped into the underground gasoline storage tanks, contaminating the aviation fuel, and there was none available for Alberto's airplane.

He went inside the air charter office and bought himself a Coke from an old bottle machine, then called the FAA to get an update on the weather. When he got through, he came back out to the flight line and stood next to his airplane, sipping on the bottle, debating with himself about what to do next. He thought of returning to Marathon, but the distance to Marathon from Key West is half the distance to Havana. By the time he landed and fueled up in Marathon it would be too late to go back out. So he decided to press on and head south, toward Cuba. I have three more hours of fuel, he thought. I can search plenty in three hours over the Stream in this weather.

northeast and follow the Gulf Stream back toward the Florida Keys.

Thirty years looking and not finding, he thought. And then you hear all these strange stories. Some of them could not be true, but some of the strangest were, and he knew that the one that he was remembering now was true because he had talked to the man and he had seen the wallet and the little red flag with his own eyes and because you could not invent so much pain.

The man had escaped on a raft made of plywood and inner tubes. The man's brother had planned to come with him but had lost his nerve at the last minute. So there, by the shore, the man said to his brother, "You are a *gallina,* a chicken. You don't have any *cojones.*" The man was trying to shame his brother into changing his mind, not really trying to insult him. The man's brother said nothing and just helped him get off, pushing him a little way into the water. And as the man drifted off, his brother waved goodbye slowly, with great sadness.

A year later this same man is working at the Flamingo Hotel in Miami Beach and he is out there picking up trash on the beach in the cool grayness before the sun rises and he sees an inner-tube raft that has come up on the sand with the early tide. And in a plastic bag tied to the raft he finds his brother's wallet and a little red flag. The man runs up and down the beach calling his brother's name and later he calls Immigration and the Coast Guard and everyone he can think of, and of course he never finds his brother. Then one afternoon in a bar in Key Largo the man comes up to Alberto, without ever having met him, and tells him his story because someone at the bar points out

Alberto and tells the man that Alberto is "the pilot who's always looking for raft people." And even though in his mind the man knows his brother is dead, his heart refuses to believe it, and when he finishes his story the man's eyes are brimming with tears and he tells Alberto that to this day he still looks for his brother when he is walking down the street, and sometimes when he goes into a *timbiriche,* a little hole-in-the-wall café in Miami, his heart leaps when he sees the back of a man's head that reminds him of his brother, or someone making a gesture like his brother used to make.

Stories like this and hundreds of others Alberto had heard over the years were the reason he kept looking. The fact that these stories (and others no one has heard) kept playing themselves out every day—every day for thirty years!—were sufficient reason to keep looking, he told himself. Were they not justification enough?

Now, very low on the horizon, Alberto saw a hint of grayness and he knew that it was the top of a hill and that soon, if he kept his heading, he would see the thin green coastline of Cuba rising from the sea. But he figured he had come close enough, and turned away to the northeast.

There was no sense in tempting them, even if he was flying so low that he was sure no radar would pick him up. Still, it was better to be careful and not tempt them unnecessarily, even though he knew that he was over international waters and that they were in no mood to create an incident with the United States by shooting down an unarmed Cessna. Not the way things had been going for them lately. Thirty years ago it would have been a different story. He would have been cockier, much cockier. And *they* would have been cockier. But that was thirty years ago. Now, at sixty, after all he had been through, Alberto did not want to confront a MiG or, rather, to become a victim of one.

The sun was lower in the west, and the Gulf Stream had taken on the colors of the late afternoon. Behind him the water was melted gold. To the east, the slant of the light had given the current a dark greenish tint that in the distance turned to a deep, melancholy violet. But visibility was still good and there was a strong wind blowing from the east that raised whitecaps and kept away the haze.

It will take longer with this headwind, he thought. But if I push, I can make it to Key Largo while it is still light. Pushing it faster will use more fuel, that's true, but I can still make it to Key Largo and search a little around the upper Keys while there's light. I'll look around as long I have light, and if I have to, if I'm *really* low, he thought, I'll put her down at Ocean Reef Club. They won't like it, being private and all, but if I have to, I'll put down at Ocean Reef.

Earlier Alberto had decided that he would just head back to Marathon and leave the search around the upper Keys for the morning, but now in the sad light of the afternoon he felt a strange urgency, a powerful need, to use every last ray of light to search for these people. And he knew that he would search well into the twilight because, without anyone demanding it or expecting it or even knowing that he was doing it, he felt that it was the right thing to do. And to feel—without doubt—that you are doing the right thing at any given moment is a rare thing, or at least it was for him, he thought. Maybe other people feel differently. Maybe other people feel that they are doing the right thing all the time as they go about their lives doing everyday things that are expected of them. But he usually started his days with a vague uneasiness, a lingering feeling that he should be opening his eyes in some other place, doing some other thing. So he savored this rare feeling of peace and communion with the world and let it dwell comfortably in him so it would settle undisturbed in his memory and come back to him later.

He had felt this same way twenty-nine years ago when he flew a B-26 over the bright waters of the Caribbean on his way to Playa Girón during the failed Bay of Pigs invasion, and since then (until today) he had never been able to bring back the sensation fully. He could remember it but not fully bring it back. The same way you can remember having been in love and everything surrounding the experience, the places you went, the things you did, everything you said. But not the experience itself. Or the colors. Each love has its own colors that spill over the trees, across the sky, and beyond the horizon into the deepest recesses of the universe, touching every planet, painting every star. And those colors can never be brought back, he thought.

The feeling Alberto had now was like touching something far beyond the everyday, like being caressed by a peaceful and eternal thing. There is no word in Spanish for that feeling, and Alberto did not think there was an English word for it either. But he could not be sure. He had not fully mastered the English language. So he tried hard to think of an English word for it.

Then he thought about the early days in exile. October 1960. Recruited by the CIA a week after landing in Miami. They were planning a mysterious large-scale operation against Castro, and experienced Cuban exile pilots were in great demand. No one told him the operation was large-scale. In fact, no one told him much of anything at all, not even that the people who recruited him were with the *Compañía,* the Company, which is what Cubans call the Central Intelligence Agency because the abbreviation *Cia.* is the Spanish equivalent of *Inc.*

But it was obvious enough. The word was out on the streets. The *Compañía* was looking for Cuban exile pilots, mechanics, navigators, certified scuba divers, anyone who could handle a boat, read a radar screen, anyone with military experience. Cuban medical personnel were also in high demand. Something was up. Something big.

Two agents took Alberto to an apartment in Coral Gables and hooked him up to a polygraph machine.

"What is your father's name?"

"Rafael Flores."

"When were you born?"

"October fourteenth, 1930."

"Are you a Communist?"

"No!"

"Are you working for Castro?"

"Of course not!"

"Are you a homosexual?"

"What?"

After he passed the lie-detector test, he spent a few days taking batteries of U.S. Air Force exams on flying theory, aircraft systems, navigation, weather. Then he went through a series of psychological tests and a complete physical examination before he was flown to a secret CIA base in Nicaragua.

The base, nestled in the mountains of western Nicaragua, had reminded him of Cuba because of the beauty of the vegetation, the deep forest greens and the vivid, iridescent colors of the flowers. But it was different, he remembered. In Cuba, even in the mountains, you can always sense the sea, and the balmy breezes of the Caribbean follow you everywhere, making the air light and sensual. In Nicaragua the mist hung over the mountains all day and there was an oppressive quality to the atmosphere he had never felt before.

After he began training with the American instructors, Alberto encountered something else he had never known in Cuba. He learned how it felt to be a stranger, a foreigner. The Americans were nice enough, but in many respects they treated the Cubans like children. Alberto had been flying since he was a teenager, and by the time he escaped he had logged almost seven thousand hours in many kinds of airplanes, but he was far from being the most experienced of the Cuban pilots. The former chief pilot of Cubana de Aviación, Cuba's national airline, was there, and there were former fighter pilots who could do things with an airplane that would eventually surprise their American instructors.

The Cubans took the condescending treatment from some of the younger instructors in stride and they joked about it among themselves at night in the barracks.

But there was something else that had bothered him and the other Cubans, and they had not joked about that. Shortly after arriving at the base, Alberto began to notice that the Cubans were being treated as second-class citizens. They were not consulted, even about matters of which they had superior knowledge. It was very frustrating to sit through a briefing and listen to a CIA agent describe what an aerial photograph shows and *know* that he is wrong and then to be ignored, as though you were a six-year-old or a blithering idiot, when you pointed out the error.

"The landing craft can't get through there."

"Why?"

"Because of those reefs. See *there* on the picture, those are *arrecifes,* reefs."

"Oh, no. Our photo reconnaissance experts say that's seaweed."

"Well, it's not seaweed. It's reefs."

"How do you know?"

"Because I've fished that area since I was a child. They are *reefs.*"

"Well, you'll just have to trust the photo experts. It's seaweed. As I was saying, the landing craft will approach this area from the southwest . . ."

Dammit, we didn't have to lose those men, he thought bitterly, packed like sardines inside the landing craft, stuck on the reefs, sitting ducks for the Communist fighters that swooped down on them, firing wing-mounted rockets with deadly accuracy.

But worse than being ignored, the Cubans began to be segregated. A sign went up on the door to the bar at the base: CLASSIFIED PERSONNEL ONLY. None of the Cubans had a secret clearance so the sign might as well have said, "No Cubans." There was no purpose to the sign other than to exclude Cubans. Alberto was furious and he decided to do something about it.

In the months leading up to the invasion, CIA pilots had been flying missions to drop supplies to the anti-Communist resistance fighting in the Escambray Mountains. The flights were at night and they had a miserable record for accuracy. The CIA pilots did not know the territory and they were coming in too high and often dropping the supplies on the other side of the mountain from where the rebels were, right into the lap of the Communists, who gladly accepted the extra help from Uncle Sam. Alberto went to the base commander to try to persuade him to allow a Cuban crew to fly one of those supply missions.

"I don't know. Those are nighttime precision drops that require much flying skill."

"Well, they can't do any worse. Besides, you shouldn't be risking American lives. This is *our* fight. You have done so much already, Commander, and believe me we are very grateful."

"I guess you're right. Can't hurt to try one mission. *You'll* be the pilot in command. Pick a good copilot. An American instructor will go with you."

The sun was low in the west, casting the long shadows of the mountain peaks across the small airstrip, when the twin radial engines of the B-26 came to life. The Escambray Mountains were nine hundred miles to the northeast, and it would be close to midnight before they arrived over the target.

Alberto had spent all day looking at the chart, memorizing every detail, making calculations in his head. He remembered taxiing the B-26 to the head of the runway and lining it up, his eyes fixed on the horizon while his experienced hands flew over the instrument panel flipping switches as his copilot called out the pre-takeoff checklist. Fuel booster pumps: check. Flaps ten degrees: check. Ailerons, elevator, rudder: free. Props full forward. Oil pressure: green. Fuel pressure: green. Ammeters, suction, flight instruments: green, green, green.

He sat on the brakes as he pushed forward smoothly on the throttles, making minute adjustments with the tips of his fingers to synchronize the props until the great World War II-vintage engines sang in harmony. It always annoyed him to see pilots who synchronized the props by looking at the RPM gauges, awkwardly jerking up and down on each throttle as they tried to line up the needles. It's so much easier to use your ears and listen to the harmonics. And the deep, overpowering baritone of the old war bird was beautiful.

An hour later a huge moon was rising over the southern Caribbean, and Alberto dropped close to the water. They spoke little. Each man was in his own world. The Cubans had something to prove, and the young instructor sitting behind them knew it.

The moon was high by the time Alberto saw the shoreline of Cuba. It had been five months since he left, but it felt more like a year, and the sight of the beaches shining white in the moonlight filled him with emotion. To his left, the great bay of Cienfuegos was a pool of silver. Straight ahead he could see the dark silhouette of the Escambray Mountains.

They crossed the shoreline east of Trinidad and followed a river valley that wound around the dark peaks. A few miles inland, Alberto veered to the left.

"You're going off course," called the instructor from the back.

"There's a radio tower around here," Alberto replied.

"I don't see anything on the chart."

"It's under construc—"

Before Alberto could finish the word, the three of them caught sight of the thin, ghostly outline of a half-completed radio tower speeding past their right wingtip. It had no warning lights.

Alberto could not suppress a smile as, from the corner of his eye, he saw his instructor searching furiously for a pen to mark the obstruction on the chart. He pulled out his own pen and handed it back without turning his head.

He then banked right and dove into a narrow ravine that meandered toward the mountain town of Sancti Spiritus, hotbed of the resistance.

As they approached the drop spot, Alberto eased the B-26 down to treetop level and the instructor tensed up, leaned forward, and tightened his grip on the curved metal rod behind Alberto's seat. In the dark, the steep walls of the ravine towered above them and they felt so close that it seemed as though you could stretch out your hand and touch them.

Alberto spotted a dim yellow light flashing ahead in the distance and called to his copilot, "Open bomb-bay doors!"

The copilot flipped the switch and the big doors in the belly of the aircraft opened with a hydraulic whine.

The B-26 came over the edge of a clearing, and as it closed in on the point of light, suddenly several other lights flashed, forming a neat V with the single yellow light at the bottom. "It's them!" yelled the instructor over the sound of the engines.

"Wait till I say," said Alberto.

The copilot raised the red safety cover and put his finger on the switch.

"*Espera,* wait, *espera, espera* . . . NOW!" yelled Alberto.

The copilot flipped the switch and several crates full of supplies, food, weapons, and ammunition dropped from the belly of the aircraft and floated, hanging from parachutes, toward the center of the clearing, coming down inside the open part of the V.

Alberto pulled up, bomb-bay doors in transit, and in a few minutes he was roaring over the sleepy town of Sancti Spiritus, where he turned south and headed back toward the sea. Over the water once again, Alberto felt like doing a victory roll. When he was twenty he would have done one. But with the self-confident mellowness that begins to swell in a man's heart during the third decade of life, he had felt it was sufficient just to think about it and savor the idea in his mind. So he thought about a nice eight-point hesitation roll like the ones he had done so many times at air shows all over the island.

By the time they landed at dawn, word had been relayed by the resistance to their CIA contacts, up to Washington, and from Washington down to the secret base in Nicaragua.

"Perfect drop! Right on the nose!"

That same day the sign on the door of the bar came down and lifelong friendships began over drinks between the Cuban trainees and their American mentors.

Later Alberto learned that the instructor who had flown with him on that mission was one of the last men to die during the invasion. The American instructors were not supposed to engage in the fighting, but during the waning hours of the three-day debacle, when the Cuban exiles were hopelessly surrounded on the beach by overwhelming numbers of enemy troops, the supply ships had been sunk, and Castro's air force ruled the air, that American instructor and several other members of the Alabama Air National Guard had climbed aboard a B-26 and headed toward Playa Girón to be with their friends.

The young Southerners flew the antique bomber into the thick of the battle in a last-ditch effort, reminiscent of the Confederate cavalry charges their ancestors made during the last days of the American Civil War: a brave, hopeless gesture, passionate and insane but full of beauty and honor. They were, of course, shot down by Castro's fighters, but not before taking a few tanks out of commission and blowing up several gun emplacements.

Now Alberto thought about those days and about his dead friends, and he wondered if that hauntingly beautiful lady he had met the other day had been one of those resistance fighters holding flashlights and forming that V at the drop point. He liked to think she was. She had said she was from Sancti Spiritus, and Alberto had forgotten to mention he had flown that air drop. It's amazing what age will do to you, he thought. The things you forget! Or maybe it was not age, maybe it was her eyes. He had been fascinated by her eyes, and now he realized that he had not felt this way about a woman since the death of his wife.

Alberto, you are really getting old, he thought. It has taken you three days to realize you are in love. Well, next time we'll have something to talk about.

Next time! Suddenly he felt awkward. Why did I have to be wearing that old shirt with grease stains on it? How did

I know I was going to run into such a beautiful, interesting woman? I was on my way home from the airstrip and stopped at a bar to have a drink. How was I to know? Do I have to wear a suit every day? Next time I'll wear a suit. No, I'll wear my new navy blazer, more sporty. She gave me her phone number. Some excuse about a function at her *municipio*-in-exile. Next time!

Alberto thought about flying that old B-26 at Playa Girón, and about the mysterious serenity he had felt toward the end of the battle, when he was sure he would never return, and he thought about his new love, and in the pleasant, muted light of the afternoon he followed the current toward Key Largo.

Chapter Fourteen

The old man had been playing dominoes in the shade before he walked over to the other side of the park as the ceremony began. It was a small crowd, mostly relatives and veterans. He was not a relative or a veteran. But he saw them putting up the flags and the insignia of the brigade around the open-air podium and he walked over to see.

Vivian had not noticed him standing next to her while a priest at the podium read the names of those who had died during the invasion. Vivian's father had been one of them. He had been a paratrooper who was machine-gunned during the first wave when his parachute became tangled in the branches of a tree and left him dangling helplessly over the *ciénaga* or swamp of Zapata, which lies beyond the fault. But she was also angry with her father for going off and getting killed, leaving her behind to grow up without him in a strange country. Jumping out of an airplane into a swamp. At his age!

She was also angry with Juan, whom she had never met and who was now intruding, disturbing her orderly life. And with the other two adrift Lord knows where, and with Fidel Castro who caused it to begin with, and with Batista who caused Fidel Castro, and with the man who blew his brains out on the air, who the hell knows why. She was angry with the whole bunch. All of them blended in her mind, the good ones and the evil ones, the innocent and the guilty. All of them men, all of them Cuban, all of them so *extreme.*

Vivian stood up, walked around her desk, and poured herself a cup of coffee. She had a feeling a long night was coming and she had promised Carmen she would be at the base. Well, not exactly. But she had promised her she would do everything possible and in her mind that meant staying at her station, behind her desk at the Coast Guard base. Carmen was a good friend and she owed it to her to stay at the base and keep an eye out. The hell with the men.

But even as she thought it, she knew that it was more than that. She could tell herself she was keeping vigil because she owed it to Carmen and she could curse the men and blame them, all of them everywhere, living and dead, for all the nights she had stayed up. And there was some justification in that. But she knew that it was more than duty to Carmen and it was not the fault of the men.

Away from the base, inland, away from the water and the smell of the ocean, an air of vigil hung over the city like the fragrance of a million tropical blossoms, as it had for the past thirty years. And if you were a Cuban living in Miami, there was no place you could escape from it. It would pull you out of bed before dawn and make you turn on the radio. It would keep you up late at night, listening. Waiting. Waiting. Waiting. Everything you did, every secret thought, every distant aspiration, was colored by that eternal vigil. Waiting for the day, waiting for the inevitable day.

This was Miami before The Fall (of Castro). Miami, *la capital del Exilio,* "the capital of the Exile," *el centro del destierro,* the gathering place of those who were banished. And no *exiliado,* no *desterrado,* no sojourner in this sweet but alien land needed an excuse for her insomnia.

For us, thought Vivian, nothing in this place is permanent, not even the grave. Turn on the radio and some funeral home is offering a special discount on "The Plan," if you sign up by the end of the month. The Plan, as everyone knows, provides that after The Fall your bones will be dug up and flown or floated back across the Straits—at no extra charge—to be reburied in *la Patria.* Like the bones of Joseph the Israelite, thought Vivian. And she imagined a flotilla of thousands of little arks filled with bones and dust floating south across the straits.

What an insane, impermanent city! How insubstantial, she thought. Everything is as liquid as a dream. A warm, balmy tropical dream where things appear out of the darkness only to vanish again in the mists. And after the dream, what remains? Nothing solid remains, she thought. Nothing that can be touched and held, only the memory of a sweet fragrance carried by the wind.

Most people, Vivian thought as she sipped her coffee,

spend their lives searching vaguely for something that was lost in the gray confusion of their childhood memories. But for us, she thought, for the Cuban-Americans of our generation, the *Pedro Pans,* the children of the "Peter Pan" flights, for us who were plucked from our world as we slept, the children who, without warning, without preparation, were whisked from the hands of their parents by conspiratorial strangers and flown across the Straits into a strange new world; and for all the other children who, like the Peter Pans, awoke one morning on the other side of the Straits, the transition was so sudden and the loss of innocence so abrupt, that in our memories the flight has assumed the trappings of a paradisiacal expulsion. And everything beautiful and distant that tastes of Paradise relates somehow to that flight. So we keep searching and waiting. For what? she thought. For the way homeward? For the return? For the source of that lingering fragrance? We keep searching, she thought, just as our crazed Iberian ancestors searched. For what? For gold? For Eldorado? For the crystal source of an eternal spring? Or the way a man searches and a woman waits for the return of an impossible love that was lost back in the place where the courses of their lives crossed and touched gently, so gently, and then forever diverged.

It had rained briefly at sunset and it was darker now but the clouds had dispersed and through her office window Vivian could still see a red luminescence with streaks of solid purple and other, more subtle colors spreading out across the sky behind the city and reflecting off the waters of the bay.

"I brought some dinner," said Carmen as she walked into Vivian's office.

"Thank you. You didn't have to go to the trouble, but I appreciate it."

Carmen came in carrying a large paper bag out of which she pulled three rectangular aluminum containers with cardboard tops. There were a couple of *palomilla* steaks sprinkled with lime juice and covered with sauteed onions in one, the second was filled with white rice, and the third had *platanos maduros fritos,* sweet fried plantains, and there were black beans in a pint-sized Styrofoam container. She also brought paper plates, paper napkins, utensils, and canned soft drinks, all of which she laid out neatly on Vivian's desk.

The two women ate quietly. After they finished they remained silent for a long time, each one with her own thoughts. Then Carmen's face became troubled as she felt guilt, like an unpleasant bile surging inside her, darkening her eyes. "It's all my fault," she said, "this whole thing."

"How can you say that?"

"If I hadn't defected, if I had stayed, if I had waited, none of this would have happened."

"They did what they wanted to do. They did what they had to do. You can't blame yourself for such a thing," said Vivian.

"But it *is* my fault. Juan would have never left if I had stayed. And now it is almost over. The way things are going, Communism crumbling around the world, soon it will be over, behind us like a bad dream. I should have stayed and held on a little longer."

"You're becoming like the rest of the Cubans in Miami,

Carmen. The infection is getting to you. According to them, it's been almost over every evening around this time for thirty years."

"Them? Aren't you one of *them?*" Carmen asked.

"*A veces,* sometimes. You just got here—you don't know what it's like every *Noche Buena,* every Christmas Eve, the same toast: 'Next year in Havana! Next year in Havana! Next year in Havana!' Every New Year's: '*¡Volveremos!* We shall return!' *Volveremos, volveremos, volveremos.* All the time, everywhere, all your life: *volveremos.* And every day *la Corriente,* the Stream, brings people across the Straits in flimsy little rafts, and *I'm* responsible for picking them up, for rescuing them—I'm sorry—I didn't mean to say that. It just came out."

"It's okay," said Carmen.

"*A veces,*" Vivian continued, "sometimes I have to get away and pretend."

"Pretend what?"

"Pretend that I'm American. Pretend to live a normal life. I go to New Hampshire, to the White Mountains, among the birches away from palm trees, and in the little towns no one talks about Cuba, no one thinks about Cuba. It's just a little speck. Come back to Miami and Cuba looms huge, hanging over the city, and it's '*¡Volveremos! ¡Volveremos!*' But of course we can never truly return."

"Why didn't you stay in New England after you graduated? Why did you come back to Miami?"

"*¿Qué iba a hacer alla arriba?* What was I going to do up there? It's not my home. This crazy place is. *¿Qué iba a hacer?* This is what I have to do. Besides, there was great pride in coming back after the academy."

Vivian remembered arriving in Miami as a *Pedro Pan,* a Peter Pan, which is what they called the children who were sent ahead to the United States by their parents in the early sixties through a semi-clandestine, visa-waiver operation run by the Catholic Diocese of Miami in conjunction with the U.S. State Department and inside contacts in Cuba. That was back when the rules of the revolution were changing every day. Parents were afraid Castro would send their children to Russia if war came and they would lose them forever to that distant, sunless place. Strange, sad things were happening in Cuba. The Communists were using schoolchildren to snitch on their parents, to sniff out "counterrevolutionaries." Many people were arrested because of an unguarded comment at dinner. There were rumors of war, of an American invasion. People whispered, "The Americans won't allow a Russian base ninety miles away. *Nunca,* never. It'll never happen. Better send the children to Florida where they'll be safe before Castro sends them to Russia. Then, if an invasion comes—and you know it will—when Cuba is liberated we'll be reunited. If Castro sends them to Russia, when the war comes, like the Communists are saying, we'll never see them again." There was a sense of electricity, a feeling like there is when a great storm is about to hit, when the sky darkens and the air becomes charged and there is a strong smell of rain.

And one day in 1961, Vivian, age seven, landed alone at Miami International Airport holding a small suitcase in one hand and a piece of paper in the other. The piece of paper said "Camp Matecumbe." An hour later she was on a bus headed to Upper Matecumbe Key, south of Key Largo.

In Cuba the night before, dinner had been very sad and quiet. After dinner her father and mother had tucked her in bed with tears in their eyes, saying things like "We just want you to be safe," and "The nuns will take good care of you," and "We'll join you real soon."

Before turning out the light, her father came back and held her and said, "Remember, the most important thing is to be brave. No matter what happens the rest of your life, you must be brave."

A month later her father escaped in a small boat. The sea was rough the night he left, and from the shore they could see the lights of the heavily armed gunboats prowling back and forth, back and forth. Her mother panicked at the last moment and refused to get on the boat. That winter Vivian spent a few weeks with her father in Miami before he left for Nicaragua to join the invasion brigade, and then she was alone again and stayed that way.

So Vivian told Carmen about these things because they were in her heart and because she thought they might distract Carmen and get her mind off Juan. But they did not, of course, and Carmen continued:

"Juan would have stayed. He was not political."

"You don't believe that."

Carmen was looking out the window, and it occurred to Vivian that she had not heard a thing. She was far away, somewhere over the water, and her words came slowly. "All he wanted was to be left alone with his stars," she said. "That's all he talked about, what he loved."

"That was just another way of escaping," Vivian said.

"Yes, but only in his mind. He would have stayed if it wasn't for me."

"Even if that's true, Carmen, would you have done it any differently?"

"If I had, he would have lived."

"You don't know he's dead."

"Please, Vivian, don't raise my hopes. You know he's dead."

"No, I don't. I've spent my life picking up *balseros*, raft people, and many of them make it."

"It's been five days!"

"Five days is nothing. Some have drifted for ten, fifteen, twenty days. Some have been picked up off Port Canaveral, within sight of the missile gantries at the Kennedy Space Center."

"What about the hurricane?"

"I told you, some have survived hurricanes. I didn't make that story up for your benefit. I wouldn't do that to you, Carmen."

"I thought, with Margarita there . . ."

"Carmen, many, many make it. You know that!"

"And many don't."

Vivian was silent for a moment but quickly came back: "I read a book about a man who was shipwrecked in the Atlantic and was adrift for seventy-six days in a small rubber life raft. Seventy-six days! And he survived. Five days is nothing."

"Juan is pretty smart. I'm sure he was prepared," Carmen allowed.

"Of course he was."

"Have you heard from that pilot friend of yours, Alberto?"

Vivian stood up, walked over to the window, and looked out over the water.

"No."

Chapter Fifteen

The wind smelled of rain, and it was darker now as clouds rolled in from the east. Juan was confused and had been throughout the afternoon. He had been hearing things, voices. And he fought his confusion and the voices because he knew their cause. I'm slipping fast, he thought, in moments when his mind was clear enough to think. But part of him felt ready to stop struggling, ready to let go of the rope and slip under the warm water.

In the morning he had not been ready. It's strange to think about death in the morning. In the evening, though, it seems more natural, more familiar, he thought. And he knew that he was becoming intimate with death in the way that a man and a woman become intimate. He no longer thought of death as an idea, or a distant event. She was real, and warm, and now he felt her arms wrapped around him, pulling him slowly, with infinite promise, toward her womb. So he loosened his grip on the nylon rope and began to slip gently into her arms.

Then he heard a voice he had not heard in a long time, a voice he had not heard since he was a child. It startled him and he tightened his grip on the rope. "I knew you would come," said the voice. "I knew you would come looking for me."

Behind the voice, in the distance, Juan heard the sound of sugarcane rustling in the wind, and he realized it was his father's voice. "I know you stayed up in the tree because you were afraid after what they did to me," his father's voice said. "But I understood and was not sad. And I knew you would come looking for me."

Juan felt his blood pounding inside his head, and he was suddenly alert. The voice had seemed so real but now it was gone and he felt the wind and sensed the coming rain.

Now, in his mind, he saw his father's face and he remembered him and thought about life on the big farm in Camagüey province before they took his father away. He remembered the big wooden farmhouse with the porch wrapped around it. And he remembered riding his bicycle on the porch, circling the house, crashing into rocking chairs and side tables and hammocks spread along the great porch like an obstacle course. And the huge flowering framboyán trees surrounding the house with fiery red and purple and orange and yellow flowers that rained on the porch and covered the roof of the house in an iridescent blanket. Beyond the trees, the green expanse of pasture with horses grazing here and there. Bright horses the color of gold, and white full-blooded Arabians and chocolate-brown thoroughbreds, their black manes and tails moving with the breeze. And farther out, in the distance, the great fields of cane, sweet-smelling, fluid, swelling and moving in waves like the sea and, like the sea, reaching to the horizon in all directions. He remembered sitting on the hardwood floor in the damp coolness of the house, the smell of leather everywhere, leather chairs, leather holsters, leather switches, his father's leather riding boots. And the kitchen with all its smells: of coffee and *arroz con pollo* and *platanos maduros;* of garlic and onions and green peppers; of guava pastries and other things baking in the oven.

And now, because it was getting darker, he remembered riding at night across the fields, his own horse following his father's horse, the wind stroking his face; dark shapes, like *brujos* and *fantasmas* and other spectral things whizzing by him in the dark. And he remembered feeling manly and defiant riding behind his father with his rifle holstered and hanging from the saddle next to his leg, thinking that perhaps other boys who hung around their mothers were afraid of things that prowled the night. But *he* was not afraid because he was Juan Cabrera, son of Don Fernando, and he was sure that as they thundered through the black fields, their saddles squeaking and the sound of the rifle holsters slapping against their horses, every dark thing that saw them or heard them was afraid and shrank back into the night as they passed. That is what his father had told him long ago to give him confidence, once, when he had mentioned—casually, so as not to appear afraid in front of his father—that he thought he saw a *brujo,* a goblin, peering from behind a tree.

Since the day they took his father, Juan had hidden these memories well; hidden them deep, the way men hide private things in secret places. But now they bubbled up unexpectedly. Without effort, without being called, they arose from the depths and filled his mind with the glittering details of his life before everything changed.

Then came the upheaval and confusion of the revolution. Going to Havana, joining the young Communist Pioneers, telling everyone his mother had been a maid in a great mansion in Miramar, that his father had been killed in the Sierra Maestra Mountains, fighting beside Fidel. Making up stories to get ahead, telling everything except the truth: that he was born to a proud, respected family who owned vast tracts of land in Camagüey, that he had been a *latifundista.*

Only Raúl had known the truth. Raúl, who was born in a tiny, dirt-floored shack on Juan's land; Raúl, whose father had cut sugarcane for Juan's father; Raúl, who saddled Juan's horse and played with him when he was bored. Only Raúl had known the truth and he had never told anyone, not even Carmen.

And where is Raúl now? he thought. Has he been thoroughly digested and ejected into the water? And why think of it in such detail? Why think of those dark, nondescript clumps breaking, dispersing, and rolling in the confluence of currents? Why was his mind filled with those silent, unseen things that are pushed and shoved and scattered in the great violent ejaculate squeezing through the Straits, and then carried by the streams around the circles of the sea?

It really did not matter now, though, because after he

heard his father's voice, death had become distant again and he could think of these things (and others) without feeling personally involved. After he heard his father's voice saying, "I knew you would come looking for me," death shrank back and ceased wooing him, and her promise of dark, forbidden ecstasies faded in his memory.

But now that he was alive again, he felt tormented by his shame, embarrassed by his life, ashamed of hiding who he had been, of having accepted the unacceptable and serving the purposes of those who had killed his father and destroyed his own soul. A spurious, ridiculous, pitiful life of dissembling, of fabricating outrageous tales; of looking away, turning away, hiding in dark corners.

"Aren't you the son of—"

"No."

"You have the same name."

"Many people have that name."

"He had a big farm in Camagüey."

"I'm from Havana."

"You sure look like him."

"I told you, I'm not his son. I never knew the man. I don't know anyone from Camagüey."

"Well, you sure look like him. I could have sworn—"

"I'm not him! I'm not his son! I'm not one of them, I tell you. I'm not one of them!"

Why? Why did he do and say such things? Why did he invent such lies and pretend to believe even bigger lies? Lies so monstrous, so vast and so transparent that no one could possibly be expected to believe them, and yet everyone pretended to believe them.

And even as he asked, he knew the cowardly root of his

debasement. But he also knew that the bone-chilling, all-pervasive fear, the *negrura* that had been his companion since the moment they took his father away, was gone now and something else had grown in its place. He felt refreshed and free. And comforted by the memory of his father, and of his father's voice: "I understood and was not sad. And I knew you would come looking for me."

Had he not finally faced the truth? Had he not finally chosen? Yes, he had chosen—and deliberately, with great pain and much planning. There had been no rashness in his decision, no sudden passion. This must count for something, he thought. This should serve as some atonement for such a miserable life. This and the constant pain.

Or was the escape just another form of cowardice? No, escape had been the logical choice, the only choice that offered hope, and it carried no loss of honor. The other choices led to accommodation, or death. How many times had he gone over it in his mind? Had Martí, the great patriot, the Apostle of the *Patria,* not spent most of his life in exile? Exile was not cowardice. There was hope in exile, and Carmen was there.

Carmen. It was good to think about Carmen. There was always a sense of resolve whenever he thought about Carmen. Maybe he would share these things with her in Miami. Maybe she would understand why he had lied all his life, she would understand and forgive his cowardice, and it would be new and different in Miami.

But the first thing was to find Raúl's brother. And what? What would he say to him? What could he say to him?

Don't think about Raúl's brother, he told himself. Think that you must be very close to land. And to sustain his resolve, he thought that perhaps if he could stand up on the water right now, on the tips of his toes, or climb a tower—even a very small tower—he would be able to see a hint of the Keys. Tonight, surely, he would see the lights—or the reflection of the lights in the sky.

Hunger gnawed at him now. Great hunger, and thirst. The open sores, brought on by the sun and salt water, that covered his face and arms and waist and crotch tortured him. He also felt horrible pain in his legs and his bare feet from the constant jellyfish stings, and deep-down-in-his-bones fatigue.

But he tried not to think of these things. He sensed that the crossing was nearly over. Or perhaps this was the beginning of another, darker crossing, he thought. Who knows? No matter, he was ready for that too. Either way, soon there would be rest.

Rest. Rest. In the end, when you no longer care, it is good to think of rest. But it was dangerous to think about rest now. It smelled of death, it spoke of death. And there was little practical distinction. Perhaps there was no distinction. So he fought this thought too, even though it was pleasant and hard to fight.

Juan was used to fighting thoughts. He had done it all his life. But now, because of his exhaustion, it became very strange when he tried to empty his mind. His head began to spin, going here and there, avoiding this, fighting that, and he became very tired and confused.

Later, in his confusion, he again heard faint sounds and voices from far away. "*Espera,* wait, *espera,*" and then the sound of thrashing in the water. "*Espera, por favor, espera.*"

He also thought he heard a strange sound coming from the sky.

Then he heard other voices that he did not recognize, and he considered these to be animal voices: the deep, awesome voices of the beasts of the sea. They called to him and offered him pleasant things, as they did in the nursery rhymes of his infancy where fish and other marine creatures offered food and drink to little boys visiting the bottom of the sea, as if this were the most natural thing.

The animal voices said, "Leave the raft and join us and you will see how nice everything will be. Come and play with us and we will sing the old songs together as we used to before everything changed."

And he began to go, following these voices. It was as if he were on land again, walking effortlessly, going to visit a friend who lived down the road. Until he heard his father's voice again, saying, "I knew you would come looking for me," and he looked up and saw the raft drifting a few feet away.

He was amazed to see it drifting away like that. Dazed, he watched the receding inner tube for a moment, then lunged toward it, grasping the rope. Summoning all his strength, he pulled himself onto the inner tube and lay facedown across it, breathing hard and shaking all over. The voices were gone. The pain was gone, and he was glad to be alive.

The wind had risen steadily and grew chill now, rippling the surface of the water. In the distance, Juan heard the rain falling on the sea, and he enjoyed the freshness of the wind and the sound and smell of the rain as it drew near. He raised his head, looked toward the horizon, and saw rain clouds scurrying across, changing shapes, tumbling into each other playfully.

When the rain arrived it felt good on his back, running through his hair and down the sides of his face. He cupped his hands to catch the thick raindrops, and lapped the water with his tongue. But it was over too soon and the wind blew the clouds to the west, obscuring the sunset. Now, above him, the sky was clear and glowed deep red. The red grew lighter toward the east, mixing gradually with subtler shades of blue and gray, until it turned a pale rose and disappeared near the eastern horizon.

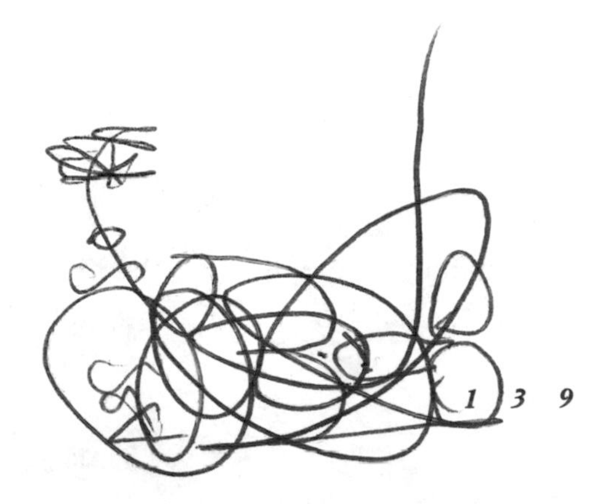

Chapter Sixteen

Alberto had flown past it, and now he was circling back, gradually increasing his altitude to gain perspective. He had sensed a sudden flash of color slipping under his left wing, one of those annoying, elusive visions reserved for the corner of the eye.

"Waste of fuel," he said out loud, arguing with himself. "I'll barely make it to Key Largo as it is, and here I go round in circles again."

But his hands paid no attention to the bickering. They banked the Cessna smoothly to the left, keeping the wingtip just below the horizon, out of his line of sight as much as possible.

At such a shallow angle of bank, the turn was exasperatingly slow. But it was better than bringing the wing down farther to hurry it up and completely blocking his vision. Everything is a trade-off, he thought. High-winged airplanes are so comfortable—ride in the shade, nice view of the ground below—then the wing gets in the way when you try to turn.

To see better into the turn, he leaned his head forward, tugging at his shoulder harness, and looked at the water through the curved left edge of the windshield. The harness restricted his movement. Should unbuckle the darn thing, he thought. But he didn't. He always wore a shoulder harness. Years of habit drilling students were hard to break.

He glanced down at the gas gauges: both needles showed empty. Must be the turn, he thought, to comfort himself. Gauges lie if you're not straight and level. It's only the turn.

The nearest field, Ocean Reef Club, was about twenty miles to the northwest, twelve minutes' flying time. Surely I have enough fuel to make that, he thought.

To the west, cumulus clouds trailed gray skirts of rain across the water, like a somber procession of old women making their way to a sad and quiet place. Earlier he had flown through some of those showers, sun setting behind him, rainbows dancing in the mist around the propeller.

Alberto looked down toward the instrument panel again, this time at the directional gyro, which was swinging back to the southwest. When the directional indicator card approached the heading of two-one-zero degrees, he leveled the wings, pulling the little airplane out of the turn. Now he was heading back in the direction he had come from. Whatever it was he had seen—or thought he had seen—

should be ahead of him, a little to the left because of the wide turn. Right where he wanted it to be.

Alberto pulled back on the throttle, dropping the nose and putting the airplane into a gradual descent. Then he stretched his hand to the right of the throttle and brought the wing flap switch down one notch, lowering the flaps to slow the aircraft while he kept his eyes on the water.

In a matter of seconds he had the airplane precisely trimmed. He let the Cessna fly itself while he swept his eyes slowly across the water, intensely searching each sector of an imaginary grid that spread out ahead of him and to his left, all the way to the horizon.

The water was the color of slate broken by the dim, irregular lines of whitecaps still showing in the dying light.

Nothing. He continued searching for a few minutes until he was sure he had, once again, flown past whatever was bobbing down there. Bobbing? Had he seen it bobbing? No, he had seen only color—a flash of yellow, he thought. The bobbing had been his imagination.

Again he banked left, turning the nose eastward. This time the turn was steeper, more impatient. The directional indicator swung fast and stopped abruptly at zero-three-zero, his old northeasterly heading along the axis of the Gulf Stream.

Alberto had leveled the wings and stopped his descent exactly at two hundred feet. But instead of retracting them, he brought the flaps down another notch to keep his speed down—barely sixty knots now.

From a distance the Cessna looked like a solitary white bird searching in the twilight over the darkened water.

Circling slowly, skimming the surface of the sea in the sad, wistful way seabirds do toward the end of the day.

It's getting too dark to see anything, he thought. Then he gave himself a few more minutes of careful searching and, satisfied he had seen nothing, pushed in the throttle, retracted the flaps, pulled back on the yoke, and began to climb, turning to the northwest, toward Ocean Reef Club. Hope they won't give me too much of a hard time for landing at their precious private field, he thought. They're so touchy about things like that. "*Bueno,*" he said aloud, "I have no choice now. It's either Ocean Reef or the water."

As the airplane gained altitude, Alberto looked at a waxing crescent moon peering between dark clouds. Then he casually glanced down toward the water again.

Yes! There it is! A silhouette, a dark lump on the water. This time he kept his eyes on it as he turned and dove precipitously toward the floating thing. He passed over it at one hundred fifty feet or so, turned steeply, and came back, sideslipping, flaps down, heart in his throat.

The second pass was a little under forty feet. A yellow T-shirt. A man! Floating facedown on something. Too dark to see clearly.

He applied power, pulled back on the yoke, and gained a little altitude, turning steeply round and round, left wing-tip pointing to the man in the yellow T-shirt floating on the water.

Alberto put his hand on the audio control panel to his right, just under the dashboard, and flipped the switch to Comm 2, the second radio, which was already on the universal emergency frequency, 121.5 megahertz. He reached down for the microphone, his hand trembling, and brought it to his lips, quickly glancing at the DME—the distance-measuring equipment in the aircraft—which was fixed on an electronic navigational aid located on the water near Key Biscayne. The device in the airplane had a digital readout giving the precise distance in nautical miles to the navigational aid. A needle on the VOR (Very-high-frequency Omnidirectional Radio) dial next to it showed the direction to the aid.

"Miami Center, Miami Center, Cessna November five-four-seven Romeo, thirty-six miles southeast of Biscayne Bay VOR on radial one-seven-zero. Repeat, thirty-six DME from Biscayne Bay VOR on radial one-seven-zero. Advise coast guard sighted single man in distress floating on the water. Will remain circling until help arrives."

"Cessna five-four-seven Romeo, Miami, roger. Got your call. Advising coast guard. Thirty-six southeast on radial one-seven-zero from Biscayne Bay. Squawk one-two-two-zero and ident, if transponder equipped. Stay on this frequency."

Alberto reached over, turned the four knobs of the altitude-encoding transponder to the assigned code, and flipped on the switch. This would identify his aircraft's location and altitude on the air traffic control radar screens in Miami—as soon as he gained a little more altitude. Right now he was too low to be picked up by their radar.

He also flipped on every available light: rotating beacon, navigational lights, anticollision strobes, even the landing light.

The captain of a Marine Sanctuary Patrol boat returning to his base in Key Largo heard the call as he passed near French Reef. He quickly located the aircraft's position on his chart, determined it was less than ten miles away, plotted a course, pushed the throttles forward to the limit, and turned to the appropriate heading. His big, powerful twin outboard engines, designed for chasing the fastest boats on the water, threw out a shower of spray as he turned.

At the same time, on a dock at the Coast Guard base in Islamorada, a crewman was casting off the last stern line of a cutter while his companion cranked up the engines. It would be thirty minutes, maybe less if they really pushed it, before they arrived at the coordinates Miami had just called in.

By now Alberto could barely make out the yellow speck floating on the water below him, so he tried something he had not done since his days working as a crop sprayer and general utility pilot on the farm in Cuba. He reached for the big sealed-beam flashlight he carried for emergencies and pointed it down at the water, as he used to do so many years ago when he flew over dark fields searching for valuable lost animals like prized breeder Santa Gertrudis and Brahman bulls that had broken out of their pens during the night.

He fixed the powerful beam of light on the yellow T-shirt and held it there as he circled round and round.

Good training for a student pilot, he thought, as he constantly adjusted his angle of bank to compensate for the wind and the drift of the current. How many times had he taught his students the common ground-reference maneuver known as "Turns About a Point"? At least once a day, five times a week, for thirty years. Okay, say fifty weeks a year times thirty, that's fifteen hundred times five, which totals seven thousand five hundred.

Seven thousand five hundred times! Seven thousand five hundred sessions of drilling the maneuver into his students' heads and eyes and hands.

"Turns About a Point," he said aloud. "Objective: To perform ground track maneuver in which a constant radius of turn is maintained by varying bank to compensate for wind drift, so as to circle and maintain uniform distance from a reference point on the ground such as a tree or a fencepost."

I should have it down pretty good by now, he thought as he looked down at the yellow speck on the water, and he chuckled. But as soon as he did that, he realized he was getting cocky. And he thought about the ancient Greek legend of Daedalus and Icarus, which he always worked into the final lecture he gave every one of his students—and especially stressed with his more advanced commercial pilots—when they were flushed with excitement after successfully completing their FAA exams.

He would tell them how, in the legend, Daedalus made wings of feathers and wax for himself and for his son, Icarus, to escape from their island prison. Before they took off, Daedalus warned his son: "Icarus, dear son, I charge you to keep at a moderate height, for if you fly too low the damp will clog your wings, and if too high the heat of the sun will melt them. Keep near me and you will be safe." But as soon as they were aloft, soaring over the brilliant blue waters of the Mediterranean, Icarus became intoxicated with the magic of flight. He felt like a god, thought he actually *was* a god, and began to climb toward heaven, ignoring his father's advice. The sun melted the wax and Icarus fell to his death.

"Icarus was the first student pilot," Alberto would say to his students. "He got cocky, he ignored his father's NOTAM—Notice to Airmen—warning of dangerous conditions, and he paid for it with his life. If you get careless, if you ignore warnings, if you fly beyond your limitations, the ground will rise up and smite you. And what happened to Icarus will happen to you. You will die, and your passengers will die."

His students would laugh nervously when he said that, but Alberto, who always had a smile on his face, never cracked even the hint of one when he gave this lecture.

Now he listened to his own advice and he asked God to forgive him for his arrogance and for giving all the credit to himself for finding the *balsero.*

In the lavender haze of twilight, where the sea and the sky intrude into each other's domains, the lights on the water mix with the lights above and share a nebulous horizon for a brief time. Looking to the west, Alberto could not tell whether the pinpoint of light under the reddish moon was a star, an airplane, or a distant boat. But each time he looked the light seemed to be a little brighter.

It was clear now that the light to the west belonged to a boat coming toward him. And judging from the distance it had covered in such a brief time, it was a very fast boat. Probably one of those Scarabs or some other similar type of boat, thought Alberto.

Each time, during a turn, that the nose of his airplane pointed in the direction the boat was coming from, Alberto would flick his landing light off and on several times. He thought it was probably an unnecessary thing to do, since the boat was obviously coming in his direction. But it was better to be sure, and if it was the rescue boat, it served to eliminate any lingering doubt that its captain may have had whether the lights he saw, low over the eastern horizon, belonged to the airplane that had made the call.

Looking at the boat, Alberto thought about the rugged camaraderie that bonds pilots of vessels and aircraft crossing wide-open spaces. He knew that he would probably never see the face of the captain of the boat speeding toward him. But he felt a strong sense of kinship and he knew that it was a kinship of the soul and that it was stronger in many ways than what he felt toward some people whose faces he saw every day.

Long after I have forgotten many of those faces, I will remember the captain of that boat, he thought. And because he was thinking of faces, trying to recall the ones he had seen during the past few days, he thought again about the face and the eyes of the woman he had met in the bar down the road from the Marathon airstrip. What was she doing there? She had never said. And why had he felt such an intimate bond, as if she understood everything about him, everything about his life, the moment he saw her?

He felt sure that she had been one of those resistance fighters holding flashlights down in the valley between the curvaceous peaks of the Escambray Mountains when he made that air drop almost thirty years ago.

Yes, that was the reason he had recognized her and had known her heart so well, and she his. And he thought that in some mysterious way, the way those things happen, their souls must have met and joined in the darkness over Escambray.

Then, because he was imagining and almost believing

outrageous things like this matter about their souls joining over the Escambray, he knew now for certain that he was in love, and that he would have to let this pleasant madness run its course and ride it out as best he could, hoping that it would end well and bring them a little happiness.

He looked down at the water and realized, for one frightening moment, that he had lost sight of the yellow T-shirt. And even though he quickly found it again with a sweep of the flashlight beam, he chided himself for allowing this distraction to enter his mind now.

It must have been the light from the boat, he thought, that reminded him of the mission over Escambray so long ago and brought his mind around to the beautiful woman from Sancti Spiritus.

On the next turn he saw, out of the corner of his eye, the powerful beam from the boat's searchlight scanning the water in a semicircle ahead of it.

Sooner than he had hoped for, the light found the man, illuminating him and the inner tube, which was trailing tattered strips of canvas and other things that showed white against the dark water and looked from the air like the tentacles of some strange mollusk floating on the sea.

I should head back now, he thought. I have pushed my luck too far already. But after all those years of searching, he knew that he would remain circling until he saw the *balsero* safely aboard the boat.

Without drifting or wavering, the boat kept the searchlight fixed on the raft below him, and even from his vantage point, Alberto could sense that the captain of the boat was no amateur. There was a calm assurance in the manner of his approach.

The boat had throttled back to idle as it came up on the raft, and now began to circle it slowly, turning to port. Alberto saw only one man in the boat, and he seemed to be leaning over the side, trying to grab the man on the inner tube with some sort of hook as the boat drifted by.

He saw the boat make two passes without success, and then the man in the boat threw out a life ring attached to a line. The *balsero* slipped off the inner tube and began to swim toward the life ring. At first he seemed to be making progress in the direction of the ring, but then he became disoriented, turning round and round on the water—probably blinded by the searchlight, Alberto thought—and he began to flounder.

The man in the boat jumped into the water, holding on to the lifeline, and swam toward the *balsero.* He reached him with a few strokes, slipped the life ring on to him, dragged him back toward the boat, and pulled himself back up over the gunwale. He then brought the *balsero* aboard near the stern, lifting him over the gunwale.

Alberto circled one more time and then began to climb as he pulled out of the turn, and picked up a northwesterly heading of three-two-zero degrees toward Ocean Reef Club.

In a few moments a new green point of light appeared on the air traffic control radar screens in Miami with a four-digit code right below it, one-two-two-zero.

As he leveled the airplane at twenty-one hundred feet, the lights of Key Largo stretched across the horizon ahead of him. On his left, the long line of lights arced gently toward the southwest: Tavernier, Plantation, Islamorada, Upper Matecumbe, Lower Matecumbe, Long Key, Marathon, Bahía Honda, Big Pine, Little Torch, Ramrod, Cudjoe, Sugarloaf, Saddlebunch, Boca Chica, Key West. In the distance, the lights turned yellow, then reddish farther out as they mixed with the lower stars near the southwestern horizon. To his right, toward the north, the sky was aglow with the awesome brightness of Miami.

It was a glorious, eternal moment. And in that moment Alberto took in the night, its darkness and all of its lights, above and below, absorbing them, like a subtle fragrance. He thought about Icarus again and wondered if, as he plummeted down to the sea, Icarus felt it had been worth it, after all. The legend is silent on that point.

The rafter was probably not with the group that Vivian called about, he thought. But that did not matter. He had found him and he had stayed. And tomorrow he would go out again, and the day after that.

Silence. Absolute, perfect silence. For a moment it seemed so natural: an extension of the darkness, part and parcel of the night.

Silence.

"Miami Center, Cessna five-four-seven Romeo. Mayday. Mayday. Twenty-four DME on radial one-eight-five from Biscayne Bay. Lost engine. Declaring emergency. Cannot make Ocean Reef. Ditching—repeat, ditching. Will maintain present heading of three-two-zero degrees until splashdown. Estimate splashdown five or six miles southeast of Ocean Reef."

"Cessna five-four-seven-Romeo, Miami, roger. Radar contact. Alerting Coast Guard. Latest wind at Ocean Reef—stand by—latest wind at Ocean Reef is zero-niner-zero at ten gusting to fifteen. Altimeter, two-niner-niner-eight. No further transmissions required from you. Will confirm current wind and advise. Stay on this frequency."

Okay now. Flaps, thirty degrees. Airspeed, sixty knots. Rate of descent, three hundred feet per minute. Cabin doors—unlatched. Life vest. Where's that life vest? Okay. Here. I've got it. Wind from the east. Zero-nine-zero at ten. I'll bring her into the wind before splashdown. Maintain present heading for now. Won't be able to see the water. Flip on landing light, that should help. It's already on. Okay. What else? Keep your head. Hope that emergency locator transmitter works. Paid good money for it. Hope it works. Should go on the minute the plane hits the water. Hope it works.

"Cessna five-four-seven Romeo, Miami. Current wind at Ocean Reef is zero-seven-zero at fifteen gusting to twenty. Altimeter, two-niner-niner-eight. Coast guard advises they have a helicopter on the way. Good luck, sir."

Wind from the northeast now. Zero-seven-zero at fifteen knots. Okay, altimeter. Dammit. Forgot to adjust altimeter to current barometric pressure. Keep your head, Alberto. Keep your head. What did he say?

"Miami, five-four-seven Romeo, I'm sorry, what was that altimeter?"

"Two-niner-niner-eight. Wind is zero-seven-zero at fifteen."

The lights were much closer now and almost at eye level, filling the windshield. At the air traffic control center in Miami, the green point of light identified as one-two-two-zero on their radar screens flickered for a moment and then disappeared.

Time to turn her into the wind, he thought. Whatever

you do, Alberto, don't stall her. Keep her flying all the way down. Keep her in control all the way to the end. Okay. Heading, zero-seven-zero. Altitude, three hundred feet. So dark down there. Two hundred feet. And he thought he had forgotten his Latin but it came back now, from his days as an altar boy such a long time ago in Santa Clara. It came back clear and mellifluous, smelling of dampness and incense, resounding off dark corners, off hollow round places way up high, so high, so long ago:

"Pater noster, qui est in coelis: sanctificetur nomen tuum: adveniat regnum tuum: fiat voluntas tua, sicut in coelo, et in terra . . ."

Dark water rushed over the windshield and he heard popping sounds as the delicate fuselage, designed for more ethereal regions, strained and cracked and ripped in places. Warm water poured into the cockpit, through open doors, through vents, through seams.

He grabbed the life vest and reached down to unfasten his lap belt and shoulder harness. Stuck. Jammed somehow. How can it be stuck? Must be doing it wrong. Must have my hand on something else. Keep your head. Okay. Feel for the buckle. I have it now. Stuck. *¡Dios mio!* This is silly. This is not the way it happens.

Why are the instruments still lit? They should have shorted out. Maybe the water has not reached the wiring. Who knows? Why am I thinking such things? Why am I thinking of wiring as if it were the most natural thing to think of now? This is not the way it happens. This is not the way at all, he thought.

But, of course, it was that way—with all the flight instruments shining before him: airspeed dial stuck on zero; the ball on the turn-and-bank indicator wobbling drunkenly back and forth, back and forth; clock still ticking; altimeter at sea level. And, in the center, the artificial horizon: that beguiling instrument pretending to represent the world, with its blue half-circle of sky on top, and its black half-circle of earth below, and its quaint little airplane flying toward a painted horizon, following perfect white lines that converge way off, way off somewhere at the center of things.

They were all there, each in its own place, looking at him like old friends keeping a silent vigil. So that in the end it was more familiar than he had thought it would be. It was not so strange.

Chapter
Seventeen

They took Juan to Fisherman's Hospital in Marathon, and Carmen drove down to be with him, but Vivian stayed behind at the base in Miami, waiting for the helicopter that was bringing the body of Alberto. The first call had come around seven-thirty and the second twenty minutes later.

Now it was nearly ten and the wind had picked up, blowing steadily from the ocean. Vivian was standing by the helipad, looking south across the bay, as she held her cap to keep it from being blown off her head by the rising wind.

It had taken divers nearly thirty minutes to free Alberto's body from the floating wreckage and hoist it on a litter up to the helicopter hovering over them.

The only thing that showed above the surface when the

Coast Guard helicopter first arrived at the crash scene had been the top of the wings and the vertical stabilizer.

The wreckage had rolled and pitched unsteadily in the swells, making the work of the divers difficult. As they pulled the body from the swaying airplane, the divers had to be careful not to puncture the fuel tanks in the wings, which were empty and the only thing keeping the aircraft barely afloat.

After they brought the body aboard, the helicopter continued to hover over the wreckage until a boat arrived to tow it back to the base, where it would be taken apart by investigators from the National Transportation Safety Board to determine the cause of the crash.

Newspaper and television reporters were already at the Coast Guard station awaiting the helicopter. Earlier, when they first got there, Vivian had radioed the pilot and reminded him to have the body fully covered and to instruct his crew to disembark with appropriate military decorum. "Remember the image of the Guard," she had said. But the pilot knew his commanding officer well and knew that although her dedication to the Coast Guard and her professionalism were second to none, this time her concern went beyond "the image of the Guard" and he respected it.

Vivian followed the blinking lights of the helicopter as it circled west and turned into the wind for its final approach. It then hovered for a few moments over the helipad and touched down precisely at the center of the circle painted on the concrete. Vivian waited until the engines were shut off and then marched slowly toward the open hatch, still holding her cap. The pilot and crew disembarked and smartly saluted their commander. Vivian returned the salute and stood ramrod-straight as they brought the litter out of the helicopter, then helped them carry it into the hangar, where it would remain until the medical examiner arrived.

That night Vivian took care of every detail personally, with her customary efficiency. She spoke with the medical examiner, filled out all the paperwork, dictated several reports, and made the necessary telephone calls.

Alberto had no children, and his wife had died ten years ago. Vivian did not think he had any living relatives in the United States, but she knew he had many friends. Some of them were mutual friends, and she called as many of those as she could remember to spare them the unpleasantness of finding out about it from the morning paper. The call to Margarita was the last one, the hardest one.

By the time Vivian got home, it was almost three in the morning. She took off her uniform and hung it neatly in the closet. Then she sat down on a chair, pulled off her shoes, wiped them with a towel, placed them on the shoe rack beneath her uniform, and stood in the closet for a few moments staring blankly at the floor. She then turned off the closet light, walked across the bedroom, and turned off the lamp on the night table. In the darkness she removed her half-slip, her bra, her pantyhose and her panties, and, feeling too drained to look for her nightgown, she crawled naked into her bed and cried for a long time.

Ninety miles south of Miami, Juan was awake in his room at Fisherman's Hospital. In the gray half-light that filtered through the crack in the curtains, he was looking at an intravenous tube taped to the back of his hand.

Carmen was asleep on an easy chair in the corner of the

room. Her body was curled, leaning on the armrest, and her legs were drawn up with the calves tucked against the back of her thighs, exaggerating the curve of her hips.

He would tell her in the morning, but first he had to sort it out in his mind. And now he was following the scent, the subtle essence of what he had lost. It smelled of leather and tasted of distant, endless fields of sugarcane swaying beyond the iridescent, blossom-laden canopies of the framboyán trees.

It had been normal, he thought at first, to give part of his life, part of himself, to them so that the rest might be preserved. Surely everyone did this. Everyone lied, everyone was deceitful and servile in difficult times: pretending, accommodating. Even in normal times, in normal places, some people take on the face of a slave, he thought. And revolutionary Cuba could not be considered a normal place, a normal time. No one would ever think or pretend it was. He had understood that from the very beginning. In a perverse way his understanding had been the pretext for his degradation. He had thought early on, *Well, I can lie, I can degrade myself. It is nothing to me. And my lies will be the greatest lies of all, I will excel in my lies. My lies will tower over theirs.* So he invented a new father, a new mother, he invented a new self and everything else. What were a few more lies in a country of liars? They were nothing. They meant nothing.

Perhaps, he had thought wryly, this was the true meaning of the "New Socialist Man." But none of this was significant or central. What was central was the blackness, the *negrura sofocante*, the *negrura impenetrable.* Because, in his case, the first time he had peered into the abyss, it was as if a gate had been opened that he could not close. And everything rushed out, everything was squeezed from him, leaving nothing there, nothing to preserve.

From the first, he had plunged into the tunnel and had spent his life running, hearing footsteps close behind and the breath of the pursuer in his hair. And after that there had been nothing else, day to day, tomorrow and tomorrow and tomorrow. His lies, after all, had been inevitable and were nothing more than that: lies. Spoken in panic, repeated in degradation.

And what were they protecting? Whom did they serve? What was at the heart of this ridiculous, elaborate wall of deceit?

He could think of nothing, he could see nothing beyond the familiar *negrura*, nothing worth protecting. And he was too tired to think about this now anyway, too terribly tired. So he pushed everything out of his mind until it became a complete blank, as he always did, and fell asleep.

Chapter Eighteen

In the shadow of Miami's skyscrapers, on a finger of land jutting into Biscayne Bay, sits a small circular chapel dedicated to the Virgin of Cobre, the patroness of Cuba. The image of the Virgin faces south. Her eyes are level, looking across the water, beyond the Straits. Lush rosebushes, with blooms of many colors, are planted on the grounds around the chapel up to the edge of the water, filling the air with their fragrance. And everything about the place, inside and outside, is bright and immaculate.

It is said in the legend that Our Lady of Cobre appeared to three desperate fishermen in an open boat during a sudden, violent storm off the coast of Oriente Province. When the Virgin appeared, the wind died, the waters were calmed, and the men were saved. After the investigation and paperwork appropriate in such cases, Pope Benedict XV declared *Nuestra Señora de la Caridad del Cobre* the official protectress of the people of Cuba.

The little chapel is a symbol and a gathering place of the Cuban exile community in Miami. On patriotic days the grounds are a sea of red, white, and blue, with American and Cuban flags fluttering together in the breeze that blows off the bay.

Sunday the wind came from the north, strong and steady, stirring the leaves of the rosebushes, carrying loose petals over the seawall into the waters of the bay, and bringing an edge of fall to the air.

There was a good crowd, filling the chapel and spilling out the open doors into the sunlight. Alberto's casket, draped in the Cuban flag, was set before the simple altar.

His friends, many of them graying veterans of Playa Girón, were up front, standing in a solemn semicircle around the casket. But most people there had never known Alberto. They came because that morning a beautiful piece about him had appeared in the Spanish-language section of the paper and, reading it, their hearts had swelled with an emotion beyond pride and grief, deeper and broader than understanding. There is no word for this feeling, in English or in Spanish. So they came bearing flags and flowers, not out of obligation or to pay their respects, as they told themselves, but because something in them, which they did not understand, read the words and made them come.

The author, Alberto's journalist friend, delivered the eulogy:

"I feel no tragedy here," he told them, touching his

breast. "There is no darkness in my heart. Today my soul is brighter than the sky and as hopeful as the wind that blows so strongly over the water."

The journalist paused for a moment to look across the bay, then continued, "Alberto was the happiest man I ever met. He taught me, without saying a word, that happiness"—he used the word *alegria,* which sounds more of bliss than of happiness—"like freedom and love and other things that truly matter, comes from here." And he again touched his breast with the tips of his fingers, pressing the surface with great care, so as not to disturb sacred things. "They come from a secret place, deep inside the soul, that no one can reach. And nothing outside of us, *nada en el mundo,* nothing in the world, can put those things there or take them away . . ."

Juan, standing with Carmen and Vivian, had been leaning unsteadily against the doorframe, looking inside the chapel. Listening, drinking in this new world, so alien and so familiar, the same way dreams are alien and familiar, without contradiction.

He stepped back now, out of the way, on the edge of the doorstep, as gray, wrinkled men with bright eyes carried the casket over the threshold and down the narrow, rose-lined walk toward the impatient hearse.

Still wincing from the pain of the jellyfish stings, Juan limped as Vivian and Carmen helped him make his way to the parking lot and into Carmen's car. Vivian left her car at the chapel and rode with them, sitting in front, while Juan sat quietly in the back, looking out the window at the traffic, as they followed the procession to the cemetery.

It occurred to him that this was the first funeral he had

ever attended. What's the point of funerals? What's the point of the whole thing? he would ask himself every time someone died. *Mi padre,* my father, he would say to himself, never had a funeral. Then he would feel a sharp pain, like a stabbing in his chest, and push the whole thought out of his mind.

At the graveside there were fewer people. And it was quiet and somber. Someone whispered that the shadows seemed longer than they had been at the chapel, but most people were silent, respecting the authority of the place.

During the ceremony a mysterious, beautiful woman in her sixties sat alone on a white bench, back in the shade, away from the gathering around Alberto's grave, with distant eyes fixed on the brilliant sky showing above a high garden wall covered with bougainvillaea.

After it was over, Vivian decided to go back to the chapel with one of Alberto's friends to pick up her car, and now Carmen was leaning against the car door, her head partially in the window, saying good-bye to Vivian, while Juan sat in Carmen's car, waiting. He was looking at a piece of paper with an address he had scribbled when he was in the hospital: *Campos Chevron 11791 S.W. 8th Street.* A nurse who came out through Mariel had helped him find it. CAMPOS CHEVRON, the Yellow Pages advertisement had read, ALL MINOR AND MAJOR REPAIR WORK—SEVEN DAYS A WEEK. Then, under that, in big red letters, ALL REPAIR WORK GUARANTEED. And under that, again in black letters, JOSE ANTONIO CAMPOS, OWNER. The word *Owner* was in fancy script, proudly appended to the name.

José Antonio Campos. It had to be him, he thought. There was no other Campos listed in connection with a gas station. He had thought of calling, but could not bring himself to do it. Just as he had not been able to tell Carmen the things he wanted to tell her.

"Can we go here now?" he asked her, handing her the piece of paper as she slid behind the wheel.

"Why? What's here?"

"I think that's Raúl's brother's place."

"Are you sure you want to do this now?"

"Yes."

They passed under a great arched gateway of coquina and drove along the water for a while, past bright images of floating buildings, like anchored balloons, threatening to break their moorings at any moment and drift south across the bay.

Then they turned inland and drove through glaring, shop-lined streets with colorful signs all ending in *-ía:* MUEBLERÍA, PANADERÍA, DULCERÍA, JOYERÍA, FARMACÍA, LIBRERÍA, CARNICERÍA, JUGUETERÍA, FERRETERÍA, GALERÍA, PELETERÍA, every imaginable *-ía.* On and on and on, across miles of endless strips of furniture stores, bakeries, jewelers, pharmacies, butcher shops, hardware stores, bookstores, galleries, toy stores, shoe stores. And, as far as Juan could see, every blaring sign, every shouting notice of sale, every "help wanted" advertisement, was in Spanish.

He smelled the air, luscious with the rich aromas drifting out of sidewalk cafés: *puerco asado,* roast pork, fresh baked bread, black beans, tropical viands, *yucca, malanga, platanos maduros.* But the dominant aroma that reached him now was of coffee, dark-roasted, sweet, ubiquitous.

And everywhere, exuberant men in white *guayaberas* were leaning with curvaceous, dark-haired women against counters that jutted out into the sidewalks, drinking thick espresso in tiny plastic cups, laughing, slapping each other's backs, carrying on a constant, rapid-fire banter in Spanish.

Juan was struck—shocked, actually—by the extent and vitality of the Cuban presence in Miami. Carmen had spoken of it during their telephone conversations, but the reality truly surprised and overwhelmed him. It was as if the Stream with its awesome force had torn off huge chunks of the island as it swept past and deposited them here, bringing all the colors, all the flavors, all the fragrances, the very air itself, together with the people who happened to be standing on these clumps of *la Patria* at the moment of disengagement. And, in the passage, nothing was broken, nothing was changed, there was not even a pause in the conversations. Or, he thought, this was like those improbable stories one hears where tornadoes pick up houses and deposit them down the road leaving every cup, every plate, every saucer in the china cabinet undisturbed.

It was as if he were looking through a fantastic window at a street that had been preserved from the Cuba of his youth, before everything changed. He wanted to get out of the car and walk the streets, go into the *timbiriches* and become lost in this mass of warm, wild, gesticulating *cubaneria,* where no one looked over his shoulder, where no one seemed afraid. But first he had to see José Antonio Campos—before eating, before drinking, before anything. Going to that service station now became an obsession, like the thing he had with the warm place in the water, Raúl's place in the water, after Raúl was devoured by the shark.

And, like all of his obsessions, this one had a metaphysical root. He was convinced (absurdly, even in his own mind) that the answer to every question, the solution to every problem, the completion of every circle was to be found, for the moment, at 11791 S.W. Eighth Street.

He thought that this might be a good time to tell Carmen the truth about himself. But then he pulled back from the brink as soon as he opened his mouth, so that only the prefatory word "Carmen" escaped, clinging precariously for a few moments to the edge of the abyss, before tumbling into oblivion.

Carmen said nothing and waited. And Juan knew that she would continue to wait quietly because she understood, in the way artists always understand, that the secret is not in probing but in waiting.

So they moved silently through the treeless, throbbing streets, through the garish exaggeration of sunlight embracing everyone and everything, reflecting off the sidewalks, off the plate-glass windows, off the sweaty bald heads of old men walking earnestly with their packages.

Farther west, the road widened and the conglomeration of nondescript little shops began to thin out. The Tamiami Canal, its surface the color and consistency of pea soup, with tall pines planted as a windbreak along the far bank, now came up on their right and disappeared into the distance as it cut across the heart of the Everglades.

"Is that it?" Juan asked, pointing to a Chevron sign on their left.

"No, it's a little farther down the road. Past 117th Avenue."

For a moment Juan thought of asking Carmen to turn back. Maybe she was right, maybe he should wait. Besides, what was he going to say to José Antonio? What *could* he say to José Antonio? That it was his fault? That he had planned the whole thing and persuaded Raúl and Andrés to go along on an insane journey that cost them their lives?

He remembered José Antonio as a little boy. Three? Four? He could not have been older than that—running barefoot around the yard of the great house, hugging dogs twice his size, chewing on chunks of peeled sugarcane. And in the evening he and Raúl and José Antonio filling a great earthenware pot with water and setting it out on the porch under a kerosene lantern and watching the beetles and moths that flew around the light and fell into the water, casting fantastic shadows on the bottom of the pot as they struggled to get out, to get back into the air and fly up toward the light. Or running through the yard in the darkness catching *cocuyos,* fireflies, putting them in glass jars with little holes punched in the lids and carrying the jars into the night like lanterns. And once, when José Antonio had said that he was going back to his house because his mother was calling him, Juan remembered replying grandly, with the stupid arrogance of childhood, that it was not José Antonio's house but the Cabreras' house because the Cabreras owned all the land as far as the eye could see. José Antonio, unconcerned with the niceties of proprietary rights, had looked at him wide-eyed and said, "Well, my mother's there. So it's my house." And that ended it as far as the three of them were concerned.

Then the revolution came and everything changed. No one owned anything. It was nobody's house. Was it his fault? Was it his father's fault? Or was it one great collective fault? Was fault even connected with it? *¿Quién sabe?* Who knows? His grandfather, Don Francisco, had bought the estate during the Spanish-American war, around the turn of the century, when land in Cuba was cheap. He called it *Finca Santa Cruz,* Holy Cross Farm. It seemed like a smart and proper thing to do: to buy that land the day he bought it. It still seemed smart and proper the day he died, fifteen years before the revolution. His grandfather had never cared who was in power in Cuba as long as they left him alone to make money, which is what he cared about. Was it his grandfather's fault? *¿Quién sabe?* And what did *he,* Juan, care about? He cared about the things inside his mind that grew and flowered in secret. And the things outside? He had always regarded those with detachment, as if he were looking at them from a great distance, saying, "It's all very interesting. But what does it have to do with me?" So he handled the world as a man who is not terribly interested in playing a board game, but feels social pressure to do so, would handle the game: "What are the damn rules? Okay, fine." Then moves the pieces with sufficient skill so as not to call attention to himself, so the other players can't say, "Well, he's not being a good sport, he's not paying attention." But not with so much skill that it becomes a nuisance and interferes with important things. The trick, of course, was finding that line. Something he had usually been able to manage. What he could not manage was his demon, the *negrura.* And he was too intelligent to consider the *negrura* a creature from the outside. He knew the *negrura* grew in his secret universe, the way death grows from life. He could not lock the *negrura* out of his house because it was *he,* Juan, who lived in the house of the *negrura.* So he had spent his life running from room to room, fleeing the *negrura.* Because where can you run to when you live in such a house? That, of course, was his great problem, but it was a private problem.

The revolution? That was not serious. Only idiots took it seriously. (Of course, there never had been a shortage of idiots, inside and outside of the island). It was just another board game, and a lousy one at that. The rules? First and foremost: lie, at all times, in all places. Repeat inane slogans. Don't think. And if *you* think, never, *never* tell anyone *what* you think. But it is much easier to make it around the board if you don't think. Those, in sum, were the rules.

Of course, to pretend that he played the game indifferently (as he liked to pretend), was in itself a lie. The truth is he played it out of terror, he played it with a gun held to his temple, and that truth filled him with shame, destroyed his manhood. Yes, it *was* his fault, and the fault of others like him. And he could not escape the shame by pretending other things.

And José Antonio? What would he tell José Antonio?

"There, there's his place," Carmen said, interrupting his reverie as she pointed to a Chevron sign on their left. "Yes, that's it, Campos Chevron," she said, easing into the turn lane.

They waited for a break in the oncoming traffic and then turned into the driveway. The bay doors were open and a lanky, dark-haired boy, who looked about twelve, was hosing down the floor of the garage that was covered with white foamy streaks of detergent. No one else seemed to be around.

Carmen stopped the car in front of the bays. The boy

looked up, shut off the hose, and walked over to their car as Juan lowered the window.

"Is José Antonio Campos here?" he asked the boy.

The boy turned toward the parking area and called out, "Papa!"

Juan followed the boy's gaze and for the first time noticed the lower half of a man protruding from the open hood of an old Chevrolet. He shuddered and felt a momentary wave of nausea pass through him. Then he stepped out of the car and walked toward the protruding legs.

"José Antonio . . . José Antonio Campos?" Juan called when he was still about twenty feet away.

"Yes," came a voice from under the gaping hood with a hint of irritation.

"I'm Juan—"

"What can I do for you?" asked the voice, still under the hood, obviously engrossed in something more pressing or more interesting than Juan.

"I'm Juan Cabre—"

"Look," the voice called harshly, "I'm getting ready to close. Whatever it is, I can't fix it today." And then, in a softer, almost apologetic tone, "Unless it's an emergency."

Juan took a deep breath. "I'm Juan Cabrera. We used to own . . ." He hesitated. "From the *Santa Cruz,* the *Finca Santa Cruz . . .*"

A very large man in blue overalls emerged slowly from the bowels of the Chevrolet. The momentary cloud of confusion that had come over him began to fade, and by the time he finished stretching to his full height, the cloud had disappeared. His eyes now brightened with recognition and a broad, warm smile stretched across his face.

"Juan! Juan Cabrera! I can't believe it! I just can't believe it!"

José Antonio covered the distance between them in a couple of strides and stood facing Juan for a moment, towering over him. Then he opened his huge arms and brought them down around Juan in a big *abrazo,* all the while repeating, "*¡No puedo creerlo!* I can't believe it! *¡No puedo creerlo!*"

He held Juan at arm's length, one hand on each shoulder, looking at him closely, taking it all in, shaking his head.

"You look like a mess. What happened to your face? It's full of *ampollas,* blisters!"

"I've been through hell—came across on a raft."

"When did you get here?" he asked Juan.

"A couple of days ago."

"*¡Dios mio!* I can't believe it, I just can't believe it!" José Antonio broke out all over again. "How long has it been since we've seen each other?"

"José Antonio, I have something to—"

But José Antonio was not looking at Juan. He had turned to his son. "Tony! Come here, there's someone you have to meet! Hurry up! Just put the hose down and come here!"

Then José Antonio's eyes caught Carmen's, as she walked toward them. "Juan, aren't you going to introduce us?"

Juan was sinking again into his private horror, and José Antonio's words reached him as the light from a star would reach him, without urgency.

"Juan?"

He opened his mouth and with great effort produced something that resembled a shriek, such as a parrot or an exotic, long-armed monkey might make as it crashes through the canopy of an impenetrable forest.

"I'm José Antonio Campos," said Raúl's brother, trying to salvage the situation as he stretched out a large, grease-stained hand toward Carmen.

Carmen grasped it, staining her own hand.

Seeing the grease on her hand, José Antonio blushed. "I'm sorry, I'm terribly sorry. I should have washed," he said. "And such a beautiful hand, such a beautiful everything!" he added awkwardly, his face deep red. Then, turning again to his son, in a loud, booming voice to regain control, he shouted, "Tony! Bring a clean rag, and the grease remover!" And, looking at Juan, "I stained your shirt too. Well, I've made a mess, haven't I? I'll get you a new one. More was lost in the war, that's what Mom always said. Remember Mother?"

"José Antonio," Juan interrupted, "Raúl is—"

But José Antonio's excitement was irrepressible, and he burst out, "Raúl! Have you seen Raúl? He hasn't called me in three months! I've been trying to get him out through Panama, paid some damn lawyer three thousand dollars, and nothing, nothing—"

"José Antonio, Raúl is dead."

For a moment José Antonio had the desperate look of a man seeking a breach in an impossible wall, a look that said, *Surely there must be a hole, a gap, somewhere a hint of sunlight I can crawl through.* Then the blunt intransigence of the words struck him, and he stood there trembling like a great silent tree.

His eyes filled with tears and he said, in a low voice, "*No puedo,* I can't, *no puedo*—" He meant to say *No puedo creerlo,* I can't believe it. But his throat had constricted and *creerlo,* a recalcitrant word even in normal circumstances, could not get through.

Juan began to say something, one of those meaningless phrases that all people say in all languages at times like this. Because, at such a time, what phrase can hold significance? But José Antonio hugged him and held him in a tight *abrazo* against his chest, sparing Juan the pain of having to force words out of his own darkness.

Standing there, pressed so tightly against José Antonio's chest that he could hear his heart, Juan thought of Raúl and of how much José Antonio's great heart reminded him of Raúl's. A big lump formed in his throat and he felt thick teardrops begin to run down the sides of his face. And without effort, without even thinking about it, he started to remove the massive crust of deceit that he had built around himself over the years. He stripped all the layers, one by one, dropping them on the ground next to his feet, until he arrived at the *negrura.* Then, looking at it squarely, he saw that not even the *negrura* was important or central.

What was important was what he had seen in the last days. And there was no adequate way to say what he had seen in the last days, except this: he had seen colors in the *negrura.* In the last days, as he drifted alone in the Stream after Raúl's death, when the *negrura* came, when she arrived dressed in darkness, he had seen tiny, fleeting specks of color swirling in her breast, like the fiery little blossoms of the framboyán carried by the wind, dancing in the wind.

Acknowledgments

With gratitude to:

- My wife Rhonda for her help proofreading the manuscript and her constant support.
- My three sons, Robert, Jason, and John for their patience and understanding.
- My dear friend, novelist Clara Rising for her early encouragement.
- My agents, Tom Colchie and Sue Herner for their faith in my work.
- My editors, Michael Denneny and Keith Kahla for their enthusiasm and professionalism through every stage of production.
- Raoul Garcia Iglesias for a terrific job of translating this work into Spanish in time for a simultaneous bilingual publication.
- Tom McCormack and everyone else at St. Martin's Press for opening the door and making me feel at home.